The SPINSTER'S SWINDLE

ARCANE TALES

CATHERINE STEIN

ISBN: 978-1-949862-29-4

Book cover and interior design by E. McAuley:
www.impluviumstudios.com

For my parents:
For sharing your love of the arts, paying for my lessons,
coming to my concerts, taking me to shows,
and giving me a gift I can use forever.

Cast *of* Characters

Lydia Weaver - a spiritualist haunted by her past

Maxwell Millerson - a man of words, sometimes the wrong ones

Adolphus Millerson - Max's father, making promises he can't keep

A street swindler - taking money from tourists

Lady Virginia Farringdon - a suffragist who suffers no fools

Miss Aramina Johnson and Lady Constance Blythe - the ladies of ILSA

Jack Weaver - Lydia's cousin, a romantic scoundrel

Tess Weaver - Jack's wife, keeping him (mostly) out of mischief

Alexandria and Phantom - small, adorable, impish

Huntington Black - Max's employer, rich as the devil

Mr. Oxley - purveyor of stimulants and sandwiches

Irving Glastonbury - some Tom, Dick, or Harry

Haskins and Mrs. Pugh - dramatis personae

Julian Carter - a dealer in favors, not cash

Lizzie Millerson - Max's sister, an artistic soul

Assorted gamblers and event attendees - trying their luck

1
HEKA

primordial god, patron of magic

LYDIA WEAVER HAD RECEIVED MANY pleas for help during her tenure as spiritualist Madame Xyla, but never before had a client been desperate enough to offer their first-born child.

She allowed herself a few seconds to study the panicked young man standing in her foyer. His handsome face featured a long, straight nose and a strong chin with a deep cleft in the center. The lamplight above revealed hints of auburn in his tousled brown locks. Wide eyes the color of a bronze halfpenny were rimmed with red, and a shadow of stubble covered his jaw. This was a man who hadn't been sleeping well.

Lydia waved her troubled client into the front parlor of her townhouse, where she now conducted the majority of her spiritualist sessions. Gone were the airy lace curtains and delicate pastel furnishings of the previous occupant. Instead, Lydia had covered the walls with sumptuous fabrics. Chairs made of dark wood and upholstered with bright velvets ringed a carpet so plush it felt as though one sank into it with every step. In the very center of the space stood an antique table, each thick leg carved into a different mythological beast. A glass orb, a tarot deck, and a teacup sat atop it.

Her client paused, his eyes taking in the decor. A curious man. Good to know. Some clients simply walked in, paying little attention to their surroundings. His gaze swept over everything, lingering long enough to absorb what he saw.

Lydia closed the door and walked regally to her seat

behind the table. She motioned for the client to take a chair across from her.

He did, turning his attention to the objects on the tabletop. "Pretty teacup," he observed. "Limoges?" He picked it up and turned it over to peer at the maker's stamp. "Ah, indeed. The Allund factory. Lovely." He set the cup down. "I'm sorry. I talk too much sometimes."

"Communication, both on earth and with the spiritual realm takes many forms," Lydia intoned, inflecting her voice with a matriarchal air. Her spiritualist sessions relied on three basic principles. Exude confidence. Make the client comfortable. Lead them to their own conclusions.

"I'm sorry about the outburst in the hall," the man continued, shifting in his chair. "My family always says I have a tendency toward melodrama."

Lydia inclined her chin, keeping her laughter bottled up inside. Yes, saying, "I'll give you anything! My pocket watch! My books! My first-born child!" was a trifle melodramatic. But most importantly, it gave her clues about the speaker. He'd offered no money or jewels, so he wasn't excessively wealthy. And he considered books to be of great value.

This fit with the ink stains on his fingers and the faint scent of pipe tobacco around him. A scholar, perhaps. His suit was clean, relatively new, and well-fitting, so he was a man of comfortable means.

"Tell me what brings you here…" Lydia let her voice lift and trail off at the end of the sentence. She never insisted that clients give their names, but prompting them in this way revealed more about them, whatever the answer or lack thereof.

"Mr. Millerson," he replied immediately. "Maxwell Millerson."

Lydia flinched. Not something noticeable to most people, perhaps, but her left hand twitched in an involuntary reaction only true surprise could cause. Rarely was Madame Xyla surprised by anything.

"A pleasure, Mr. Millerson," she said. "What can I do for you?"

Millerson. The name rolled about in her brain. He could be no relation, this young man, but if he were…

If he is, you should send him away. Helping that family is the last thing you want.

Highly unprofessional, though. And if this man did have a connection to Adolphus Millerson, he might be the path to retribution.

Lydia's thoughts so preoccupied her that she nearly missed his reply, something she hadn't done since the earliest days of her career. She snapped her focus back to her work.

"Nowhere to turn," he was saying. "No one I could ask for help. But a friend highly recommended you, and I was at my wit's end, as I'm sure you can tell."

She gave him another small nod.

"I'm in something of a… situation," he went on. "Family troubles." He paused. "Do you need details? I've never consulted a spiritualist before."

Lydia gambled based on what she'd seen of him. "Your reading relies on focus. Speak as little or as much as you like, in whatever manner will lead you to center on your true question."

"Ah. Right." He paused a moment, then went on, as if to himself, "An Egyptian theme. Why? The club was making a steady profit. It didn't need an update. And now there's nothing. Less than nothing. And I don't know what to do." Millerson blew out a long breath. "There. I'm focused. Now what?"

Beneath her layers of satin and velvet, Lydia's pulse began to accelerate. The Curiosity Club. Reported to have undergone a stylish redecoration. He was one of those Millersons! Lydia picked up her tarot deck and began to shuffle. She wanted that club. She wanted it either in her possession or burned to the ground. Both were acceptable. And this chatty young scholar was her entrance ticket.

"Let your body relax," Lydia counseled. "Breathe deep. The cards will speak to your situation, and reveal a path forward."

Millerson closed his eyes briefly and took a deep breath. "I'm willing to try anything, at the moment."

Lydia forced her desired card into the fourth position at the top of the deck. "Let us begin."

Millerson straightened his shoulders and laid both hands flat on the table. "I'm ready."

Lydia turned over the top card. The nine of swords.

"Oh, swords," her client said. "Is that bad?"

She allowed herself a small smile. "You are feeling the conflict. You are coming from a place of stress and anxiety."

"Undoubtedly," he replied.

"These feelings have long haunted you. Swords, though, have a double edge. You fear the worst. Yet you have clung to a glimmer of hope. All is not lost." She flipped a second card. "The ace of coins."

A card of opportunity. A satisfaction grew inside her as she gazed down upon it—in an upright position from her vantage point. This meeting today would be her opportunity to seize her chance for revenge long sought.

"It's upside down," Millerson observed.

"A reversed position," Lydia confirmed. "This second card speaks to your present troubles. A poor investment has been made, resources squandered."

"My father," he muttered.

Lydia added this new piece of information into her reading. "He places these troubles on you."

Millerson's eyes lifted to stare into hers, the bronze color gleaming with intensity. "So what can be done about it?"

"Your third card. The future." She turned it over. "The knight of wands. Change is coming. A new adventure. If you are fearless, it could lead to great things."

"Fearless." He rocked back in his chair. "That's not especially helpful, unfortunately."

Lydia's mouth turned up slightly at the corners. "Then let us see what advice the cards give us as you seek this future."

Setting the remainder of the deck aside, she presented him with the card she had chosen. The Lovers.

"Ah." His dark eyebrows arched. "So I'm to distract myself from all my worries by indulging in pleasures of the flesh? A time-honored tradition."

Lydia's smile grew. Millerson's irreverent sense of humor meshed well with her own. Too bad he was an enemy.

"The card speaks of a partnership, not necessarily of a romantic nature. To find the peace you seek, you must be open to cooperation. Look for the one who will join you."

His expression turned serious, his lips compressing. "Where and when will I meet this partner?"

"The cards do not speak so directly. But fear not. You will know your partner when the time comes."

"Well." He mulled over her words for a moment. "Thank you, Madame Xyla. If nothing else, you have given me a few moments of distraction and entertainment, and I find myself feeling far better than when I entered your home. This is all very interesting, this spiritualism business." He waved a hand over her desk. "Perhaps we will meet again."

"If the fates so choose."

Fate had nothing to do with it. They would meet again, and soon. And one way or another, the Curiosity Club would be hers.

2
SET

instigator of confusion

GILDED PALM FRONDS. Father had spent the investors' money on gilded palm fronds. Max shielded his eyes as he stepped into the Curiosity Club's main card room. The corridor had been bad enough. He didn't want to see what damage had been wrought here.

Steeling himself, he straightened up and gazed about the room. The renovations were skillfully done, if in poor taste. No peeling paint or irregular lines. A neatly symmetrical design. Well-placed gas lamps to brighten the space.

Perhaps too many gas lamps. The once-stately room had become a glaring preponderance of gold. Gold painted chairs. Gold-framed mirrors. More goddamned gilded palm fronds.

The walls, previously smooth and unobtrusive, now boasted two-foot diameter pilasters, carved floor to ceiling with hieroglyphs. Painted scenes in mock-Egyptian style covered the spaces in between, depicting men playing at dice and cards. In the center of the room stood a fountain of a sphinx, spewing water from its mouth. Half-a-dozen sarcophagi that Max sincerely hoped were not real had been propped up in strategic locations.

Max muttered an oath and leaned against one of the pilasters framing the doorway. Did the hieroglyphs mean anything? Perhaps, if they'd been copied directly from photographs of an actual Egyptian temple. More likely, though, they'd been carved at random, in whatever pattern the designers thought looked good.

If he'd been one of the workers and happened to know how to decipher hieroglyphs, Max knew what he would have written. *Max carved this temple for the glory of himself, but mostly for the twenty-six shillings five per week.*

He turned away from the garish decor and headed for the exit. He'd seen enough. Even if they sold off every stick of furniture in the building, they'd never come up with the thousand pounds owed to the investors. Not unless the club's patrons had a full week of unusually bad luck at the gaming tables. Asking the dealers to cheat to achieve this end wasn't an option. Max's father might play fast and loose with other people's money, but he abhorred card cheats. The man had a warped sense of honor.

That was it, then. Unless Max could spin gold out of straw, in one week's time they'd have to sell the club.

As he stepped out into the fresh spring air—or as fresh as it ever got in the heart of London—he mulled over the advice the spiritualist had given him the day before. Perhaps finding a partner truly was the solution. Surely some rich toff would have a thousand pounds to spare. Max could offer a lifetime membership to the club. And the chance to name a character in the next M. M. Irgrimm play. He had a week to find someone and prove Madame Xyla a genuine seeress.

Max turned down the street and froze. "Speak of the devil."

There, barely ten yards off, was Madame Xyla in the flesh, standing beside a small cluster of tourists and a confidence man running a shell game.

Yesterday she'd worn sumptuous reds and golds, matching the decor of her seance room. A smart move, Max had thought. It presented her not so much as a person, but as part of the atmosphere. Merely a conduit for the spirits she claimed to contact.

Today, she wore a simple, modest, dark blue dress. Another

way of blending in, perhaps? But this time with everyone else on the street.

Thinking to shoo the con man away before he completed his swindle, Max walked toward the group. His eyes remained on the woman in blue. No thick black curls draped from beneath the pale blue turban she wore. In fact, as Max neared, he could see tiny wisps of blond just at the edges of the headpiece. Maybe he was mistaken. Maybe this wasn't Madame Xyla, but a woman of similar height and build.

Then she glanced at him and smiled.

Max's heart skipped a beat. She had *not* smiled at him like that yesterday. Then, she'd been formal, distant. This smile was intimate. Enticing. He moved toward her as if ensorcelled.

"Come to watch the game?" she asked.

This was absolutely the same woman. No kohl darkened her lashes, no rouge covered her pale cheeks. But there was no mistaking those captivating blue eyes with the small brown fleck, or her pretty, heart-shaped face.

"Come to save you from a scam," Max replied.

Madame Xyla chuckled. "Very gallant of you, but I don't need assistance." She turned back to the game, watching as one of the tourists made good on a small wager.

Max inched closer, his body still entranced by that come-hither look she'd given him.

Take care, he cautioned himself. He was an amateur student of human nature, but she was a professional.

The confidence man started up his game again, chatting as he placed a pea beneath a shell and began to shuffle. His movements were smooth and effortless. Swift, but not impossible to follow. When he stopped, the group began to chatter excitedly.

"Number three," one man declared. "It's definitely underneath number three."

Another nodded.

"Who would like to place a bet?" the scammer asked.

"Five shillings on number three," the first man declared, counting out coins.

"Ten on number three," someone else added.

The scammer smiled the same cheery grin he'd worn since the game began. "Excellent." He reached for the third shell.

"One moment," Madame Xyla interrupted.

The con man paused, hand still in the air.

"I'd like to place a bet." She plunked down a gold coin.

The crowd gasped, but the spiritualist wasn't done. She set down another and another, until five gold sovereigns sat stacked beside the middle shell.

"Five pounds on shell number two."

The con man's smile morphed into one of undisguised greed. "Certainly, madame. Shall I reveal your shell first, or that of the gentlemen?"

She waved a hand. "Them first, if you please."

"Of course." He turned over the third shell. No pea. "Terribly sorry, gentlemen. Better luck next time." Eyes gleaming, he reached for the next shell.

"Allow me," Madame Xyla said.

"If you wish, madame."

The spiritualist slowly tipped the shell backward. Sitting on the table where it had rested was a pea.

The con man reared back in surprise. "You cheat!"

"Do I?" Madame Xyla inquired. "I don't think so." She flipped over shell number one, which was also empty. "Three shells, one pea. Here it is. Unless you're trying to say that *none* of the shells held a pea? In that case, sir, *you* would be the cheat." She scooped up her coins. "My five pounds, please?"

"No," the con man spat.

She gestured to Max. "Shall I have my friend here summon a constable, then?"

The swindler hesitated a moment, then his shoulders sagged. "Fine." He dug into his unusually deep pockets and counted out five pounds in assorted coins. Madame Xyla made a careful study of each coin before she picked it up.

"Thank you, sir. Perhaps find a different location for your game in the future."

The con man scowled, gathered up his things, and stormed away.

Madame Xyla handed five shillings to the first bettor, and ten to the second. "Your money, gentlemen. Have a nice day." She walked off with the same air of supreme competence she had exhibited in her professional guise.

For several moments, Max stared after her, as stunned as the other men by what she'd done. Then he broke into a run.

She'd taken a confidence man on the street for five pounds. If she could do that, she could do anything. Madame Xyla was the partner Max needed.

3
FETKET

patron of bartenders

MILLERSON HAD FOLLOWED HER. Lydia let out a relieved breath. She'd had to beg a favor of a less-than-trustworthy old acquaintance to ensure a scam artist would appear on the right street at the right time. If the stratagem had failed, her promise would have been for nothing.

Well, not quite nothing. There was always a chance the man with the shell game had learned his lesson. One more small-time crook off the streets would be good for everyone.

Lydia turned up Henrietta Street toward the Covent Garden market. She and Millerson would go unnoticed among the crowds, and she could grab a bite to eat at the same time.

"Excuse me!" he called from behind her.

She slowed her pace to allow him to catch up, and they fell into step side-by-side.

"I'm terribly sorry, Miss, uh…"

"Weaver," she supplied. "Lydia Weaver." She gave him an arch smile. "Have you come to accuse me of cheating?"

"What?" His eyes widened slightly. "Oh, no. I thought it rather impressive, how you beat that fellow at his own game."

She inclined her head. "Thank you."

He rubbed a hand over his jaw. He'd shaved this morning, but the dark circles below his eyes remained. Still troubled.

"Allow me to be frank, Miss Weaver," Millerson said. "I am in need of a partner. One with the skills necessary to earn a great deal of money in a short amount of time. I was hoping you might be such a person."

Lydia gazed at him in silence, as if considering his words. Millerson was not a man who hid his emotions well. He stuffed his hands in his pockets and shifted his weight from one foot to another.

"Follow me, sir," she replied. "I know a place where we can talk."

She led him further on toward the market, where the streets grew clogged with traffic, both vehicle and pedestrian. Lydia picked her way across the street, careful to avoid soiling her shoes or the hem of her dress with muck. The air here hung thick with the mingled scents of horse manure and roasting coffee, the pleasant and the unpleasant vying for dominance.

Lydia pushed open the front door to a small shop with a carved wooden sign declaring, "Oxley's Coffeehouse." A bell on a rope tinkled.

"Uh…" Millerson followed her, pressing closer than propriety dictated. "I thought women weren't allowed in coffeehouses," he whispered.

"Miss Lydia!" Oxley himself called to her from behind the counter. "Come here, my girl. Good to see you!"

Lydia greeted the proprietor with a firm handshake and a warm smile. It had been too long since she'd visited. Oxley sported a few more wrinkles in his golden-brown skin, and his shock of white hair was a touch thinner, but he retained all the vigor and cheer she'd known since she was only knee-high.

She placed a coin on the counter. "Two of your best, please, for myself and my friend. And a pair of sandwiches as well."

Oxley took the coin. "Coming right up. I believe your usual place is open."

"Thank you."

Lydia led Millerson to the narrow corner booth where she customarily sat. It was dark, the wood worn, and the seat hard, but it gave her a full view of the room and wasn't too far from the counter. There had been nights when she and Jack had slept curled up in this very booth, when they'd been teenage orphans with nowhere else to turn.

Now, she was clean and well-fed. Wearing fine, if simple, clothing. But still as much of an oddity as always among the working-class men who patronized Oxley's shop. Several of those men had shifted their chairs to look at her, their faces twisted in frowns of suspicion.

"You are correct, sir," Lydia informed her companion. "Women are not, as a rule, permitted in this coffee house. But I am an exception. Mr. Oxley was a friend of my father." She didn't glower at the men staring at her, but neither did she avoid their gazes. One-by-one, they shrugged and returned to their conversations. They were here for lunch, not trouble, and they knew if anyone raised a fuss, Oxley would throw them out.

"Ah. Yes. I see." Millerson set his hat and gloves aside and folded his hands atop the table. "Please forgive me, I have yet to introduce myself. My name is Maxwell Millerson. You no doubt observed me coming from the Curiosity Club earlier. My father is Adolphus Millerson, owner of the club."

Lydia nodded. Many people failed to recognize her as Madame Xyla, but in this instance she couldn't tell if Millerson truly didn't know her identity or if he was lying. His already anxious demeanor made his thoughts more opaque than they might otherwise have been.

"Pleased to make your acquaintance," she replied. "Tell me, what is it you believe I can do for you?"

He took a deep breath, then spoke in a rush. "I need to raise a thousand pounds by Thursday next."

Today was Friday. One thousand pounds. One week. That certainly explained his desperation, especially when she doubted he earned more than two hundred pounds in an entire year.

"You earned five pounds in thirty seconds," he continued. "It gave me hope that there was some way... I'm sorry, I'm being terribly presumptuous, but I am genuinely at a loss. If you could provide me with some tips or advice, or suggest a quick investment, or anything at all, I would be forever grateful."

Lydia pondered his words, and this time her pause wasn't merely for effect. One thousand pounds was significant. If she did nothing, the club might well fail. Would it be enough, though? Would it be the total destruction she longed for? And then there was the possibility Mr. Millerson might find someone else to help him. Lydia was far from the only person capable of earning a quick bit of cash.

"It's not impossible, what you're asking," she replied.

He nodded. "I know. I've seen men at my father's clubs earn more than that in a single night."

That's because your father is too avaricious to pay for dealers who can catch cheaters. He buys up clubs, runs them into the ground, and then sells the remnants. And yet somehow he's managed to avoid a total collapse.

That settled things. Leaving the thousand pound debt wasn't enough. Adolphus Millerson would find some way out of it, as he'd done in the past. His fall needed to be bigger, more memorable. Something that would be talked about from the East End slums to the mansions of Belgravia.

"And I'm secretary to Huntington Black," the younger Millerson continued, once again supplying more information than Lydia had asked for. He was remarkably helpful, this young man. Too bad his father was such a piece of shite. "Some of his investments have produced significant returns in a short time." Millerson's face twisted in a moue of distaste.

Seemed he had no great love for his employer. Understandable. Black was famous—or perhaps infamous—for the shrewd investments that had made him one of the wealthiest men in London. Investments of a magnitude that would be well out of reach for a mere secretary.

"But those are rare exceptions, and I can't rely on luck in this case. I must obtain that money," Millerson finished.

Oxley approached with their coffee and sandwiches. Lydia

accepted her cup and inhaled deeply, letting the rich aroma fill her nostrils and sharpen her thoughts. She took a healthy sip before speaking again.

"I believe I can help you."

Millerson's tense shoulders dropped and his jaw unclenched.

"But first," Lydia cautioned, "we must discuss the matter of what I will receive in return."

He immediately tensed again. "I have very little to offer, I'm afraid."

She didn't doubt that. Black was reportedly a stingy employer. The two hundred a year she'd guessed at earlier was likely an overestimate. If Millerson kept himself appropriately well-attired, with a flat in a respectable neighborhood and the staff necessary to keep it clean and keep him fed, he likely had nothing left to spare.

Which explained his preposterous "first-born child" offer. Lydia wondered if he'd seen the new M. M. Irgrimm play that was running, the latest in the playwright's fairy-tale series. Millerson struck her as a theatergoer.

"I don't own much other than my pocketwatch and my books," he admitted. "If you were a man, I could offer you club membership, but…"

"I don't need a membership," Lydia replied. "But I do need entry. If you can get me into the Curiosity Club, I'll consider the debt paid."

"Get you inside?" A puzzled furrow appeared in his brow. "Like a tour?"

"A tour would be excellent. But I also want access during operating hours. If you want me to earn you the money, you'll need to allow me to participate in club activities."

His frown dissolved. His bronze eyes assessed her with an intensity that made her skin heat. "You mean to gamble your way to the money."

Or cheat, if necessary. But if Adolphus Millerson ran the Curiosity Club the way she suspected he did, she would only need to work her way into a game with the high rollers. Winning money from a pack of rich drunkards would be child's play.

"Is that a problem?" she asked.

"No," he replied, after a slight hesitation. "It's not."

"Good." Lydia lifted her coffee in salute. "To a profitable partnership, Mr. Millerson."

He lifted his mug in return. "Thank you, Miss Weaver."

Lydia took another sip. The warm, stimulating drink was a perfect complement to her growing sense of purpose.

And here's to my coming victory.

4
GEB

*god of earth, his laughter was said
to create earthquakes*

The sight of the ridiculous renovations made Max wince, even though this time he was prepared. The garishness he could handle, but it was all so wasteful. And he couldn't abide wasteful. Sometimes he wondered how he could possibly be related to the rest of his family. His father was the worst offender, but Max also remembered his sisters regularly overspending their allowances and his father laughing about it. The oldest three had married sensible men, fortunately. These days Max only had Lizzie to worry about.

"Welcome to the Curiosity Club," he said to Miss Weaver. He presented the foyer with a wave of his hand, as if unembarrassed by the decor.

Everything will work out. Miss Weaver will help me earn the money I need and Lizzie will be safe.

The reminder of the plan brought a smile to his face. Miss Weaver would win money at the club to pay the club's debts. Poetic justice, to be honest. Especially if it meant his father bought a few less Egyptian antiquities of questionable provenance.

Max assumed she didn't mean to win the entire amount here. That would ruin the club as surely as not paying the investors, and then why would she be helping at all? There were plenty of other clubs around to visit. Hopefully he didn't have to figure out a way to get her into all of them.

Miss Weaver took her time studying the entrance

hall. Already her assessing gaze had become familiar, even comfortable. She might not be here in her Madame Xyla persona, but she was still a consummate professional. Max had slept better last night than he had in weeks, and it was all due to Lydia Weaver's aura of competence.

It was alluring, that competence. It made him want to understand her. How had she become adept enough to out-con a con man? How had she learned to read people to aid in her fortune telling? Max itched to uncover all her secrets, from her reasons for wanting entry to this club to what she wore beneath her sensible dresses.

He took a step away from her to stave off any further prurient thoughts. Yes, she was a striking, interesting woman. But the last thing he needed right now was any sort of romantic entanglement.

"The card room is this way," he said, leading her down the hall and opening the double-doors for her. "This room and the bar below are our public spaces. Anyone can come in and buy drinks or play at cards. Nominal entrance fee. We keep a list of cheaters, drunks, and others who have caused trouble, but it's small. Few people are denied entry."

"Few *men*," Miss Weaver corrected. She strode into the center of the room, stopping beside the fountain and looking around.

"Women are not *entirely* barred," Max explained. "But those who come to the club are not here to gamble."

He stopped himself before the conversation could veer into even more inappropriate territory. Spiritualists were respectable women. One did not engage them in discussions of prostitution. Nor did one give them tours of gambling houses, but these were desperate times. Max would simply have to make everything as proper as possible under the circumstances.

Miss Weaver circled the fountain, then began to move about the room, pausing here and there. She made no comments on the decor. In fact, she didn't appear to even be looking at it. Instead, she studied the layout of the room, and the arrangement of chairs and tables.

"This is excellent," she declared, returning to stand beside the fountain. "This fountain is perfect."

Max blinked. "Perfect" was about the last word he would have used to describe the ridiculous water feature. "Grotesque" would have been more accurate. Water gushed from the sphinx's mouth, as if it had a perpetual stomach ailment. The tiled basin in which the creature rested was a garish combination of bright orange and a yellow-tinged green.

"I sincerely hope it's not painted with arsenic," he sighed.

Miss Weaver peered at the fountain. "It probably is. It's the correct color to be Scheele's Green."

Knowing his father, she was probably right.

I suppose we'll have to put up little signs. "Poisoned water. Drink at your own risk." Not that the drunkards who would try to drink from a decorative fountain were likely to read.

"This decor is new?" Miss Weaver inquired.

"Finished this past week, apparently. A month ago when I was here, it was all… normal."

Her gaze lingered on him. "You're not here regularly, then?"

"No. I usually only check on the finances." Max rubbed his temple. "It's my father's club, and honestly, I'd rather I had nothing to do with it."

Max turned quickly toward the door. Why had he said that? He didn't need to go exposing all the sordid details of his family situation. He only needed her to help him raise the money. But, as happened all too often, he'd said something he oughtn't. He was so much better with words on paper.

"Shall we continue on?" he hurriedly added. It came out more a command than a question, but Miss Weaver thankfully didn't argue. Max escorted her back into the hall, then up the stairs.

"Are any of the regular patrons likely to recognize you?" she asked.

"I don't think so. Why?"

"I will need you to accompany me, and it's better if you're not well known."

Max paused halfway up the stairs. "I'm not a good hand at cards. I won't be able to contribute to the cause."

"Not a problem."

A knot of anxiety tightened in his stomach. Miss Weaver had a plan, clearly, and it involved him. He couldn't say that was entirely unexpected. But thinking about it, wondering exactly what she might have in mind, made the entire situation more real. "What am I going to do?" had become "I'm doing it."

"So, uh, up these stairs is the members only part of the club," he said, trying to maintain as normal a demeanor as possible. "Members can buy a monthly or a yearly subscription. The small bar upstairs provides more expensive and higher quality drinks, including absinthe."

The absinthe was the only real reason Max had visited the club during business hours. He had a fondness for the anise-flavored green drink, but too often it was diluted, adulterated, or poorly made. Drinking only what came from a reputable source staved off any fears of dangerous or hallucinogenic reactions.

"Hmm," Miss Weaver murmured, again assessing him with her piercing blue gaze. He wished she'd look elsewhere. That stare made him feel undressed, no matter how many layers he was wearing.

"There are two smaller card rooms here where members can play private games."

"House takes a percentage of the winnings?" she inquired.

"Yes." Could that be her plan? Win money from rich toffs in a high-stakes game? Audacious. But from what Max had seen of her, she might well be up to the task. "We also have several sitting rooms where men can drink, smoke, and talk. A meeting room for holding events or—"

Max entirely lost his train of thought when he pushed open the door to the first card room. His mouth fell open. The walls had been repainted to resemble enormous stone blocks, like those used to construct the famous pyramids. In the center of the room, where a perfectly serviceable card table had once stood, lay an enormous stone sarcophagus. Its lid had been replaced with a rectangular glass tabletop.

"Oh, bloody hell," Max blurted. Dammit. He should have examined all the rooms before giving this tour. "I'm so sorry. I haven't seen this before and I wasn't prepared…" He took a step into the room.

Please don't let there be a mummy in there. Please don't let there be a mummy in there.

Miss Weaver followed him into the room, making a small noise of amusement as she took in the ridiculous table. Max took another step toward it. A third. Steeling himself, he looked down.

There was a mummy inside. An obviously fake mummy, wrapped not in the usual way, but with its arms free. Arms that held a hand of cards fanned out in front of its face.

Miss Weaver made a choking sound.

Max whirled to face her, words of apology forming in his mind that surely wouldn't come out the way he wanted them to. Their eyes met. All the words vanished into the aether. For a long moment they stared at one another.

Then Miss Weaver burst out laughing.

Max's facade of responsibility and seriousness cracked. He began to laugh too. A mere chuckle at first, but growing longer, louder, until tears formed in the corners of his eyes and his side began to ache. When had he last laughed like this? Had he ever laughed like this?

Miss Weaver clutched both arms across her abdomen,

shaking. "That is the most ridiculous card table I've ever seen," she gasped.

Max nodded, trying to regulate his own breathing. "A glass card table is absurd on its own. But this?"

"No one will want to play in this room."

"True. But they might take one look at it and decide they need another drink!" Max ran a hand through his hair, still laughing. "I don't think I want to see the other rooms. It might do me in."

"That could be what happened to our card-playing friend." She gestured at the mummy.

"Best to head back down, then. It's not safe for a body here. I hope you won't be too disappointed if we cut our tour short?"

She sobered instantly. "I've seen what I needed. Thank you, Mr. Millerson, for the visit. I would like to begin the real work tomorrow night. I will meet you outside at ten p.m. I will be dressed quite differently. I'll wear a white rose to identify myself."

"A white rose. I'll look for it." It didn't matter what she wore. He'd recognized her without her Madame Xyla garb, and he expected he'd know her even with a false moustache and trousers.

Max offered his arm to escort her out. The gentle brush of her fingers sent a tingle up his arm. Altogether too intriguing, this woman. Fortunately, he only had to see her for a week. Then he'd have the money he needed and his life could return to normal. He could survive a week.

"Thank you very much, Miss Weaver," he said to her when they reached the front door. "This means so much to me. I am in your debt." He gave her a deferential bow. "I will see you tomorrow evening."

"Tomorrow." She smiled, then turned and strode away, all grace and confidence.

Max watched her head down the street until she was out of

sight, wondering what tomorrow might bring. A thought that had been prickling at the back of his mind wormed its way out.

What the devil is she *getting out of this bargain?*

5

IAT

goddess of milk and nursing

Max stuffed his hands in his pockets and leaned against the rough stone wall. The Curiosity Club was doing brisk business tonight. It seemed the Egyptian-themed renovations hadn't scared anyone off. Yet.

He scrutinized every man who walked past, looking for a woman in disguise with a white rose in her lapel. So far nothing. Everyone was too tall, too slim, too old, too hairy, or any number of other descriptors that did not fit Miss Lydia Weaver. If she'd slipped past, she had to be well-concealed indeed.

He paused to check his watch. Three past. If she wasn't here yet, she would be at any moment.

"Hello, handsome," a low, sultry voice murmured.

Max flinched and looked up. Blue eyes with a brown patch in the right one. A heart-shaped face. A white rose tucked into a riot of tumbling red curls.

"Looking for a companion for the night?" Miss Weaver purred.

Bloody hell.

He made an effort to concentrate on her face and not on the upthrust breasts that threatened to spill from her scarlet dress. Only to fail in his attempt when she wiggled closer.

"Miss Weaver," he wheezed. "You... surprised me."

"Lydia," she corrected, leaning so close he could almost see down her dress. "No formality tonight."

"Lydia," he repeated, her name tasting like honey on his

tongue. Sweet. Wild. And not to be touched unless he wanted to be stung. "This was not the scheme I was expecting."

She cupped both breasts. "These do not fit well under men's clothing," she whispered.

"Oh, there are techniques for wrapping and for altering clothing that they use in the theater when..." Max trailed off when he realized he was still staring at her décolletage. "Never mind. Let's go in."

Miss Weaver—Lydia—took his arm. "Can you play your part?"

The part of a gawking, randy man? Yes, he could play that quite well. He nodded and they entered.

The man at the door recognized Max by sight and pulled aside the rope blocking the stairs to the members-only floor. Lydia tossed her false red curls, hiding her tiny head shake.

"Thank you, but I'm playing downstairs tonight," Max said.

The doorman didn't reply, simply replaced the rope and returned to his duties.

As they stepped into the main card room, Max slipped an arm around Lydia's waist and pulled her against him. He pressed his lips to her ear as if kissing her.

"What's the plan?"

She turned into him, putting a hand to his chest. If she noticed his sharp intake of breath, she didn't let on. Leaning close, she murmured, "How much money do you have?"

Max fumbled in his pockets, eventually producing two pounds, six-pence in various coins.

Lydia plucked the coins from his hands and swished over to the banker's counter to exchange the money for playing tokens. She caught Max's eye and gave him a flirtatious smile. "You're going to do so well tonight," she cooed, presenting him with the chips.

Did she really mean for him to do the gambling? There

was a certain logic to it. Women didn't play cards here, only accompanied the men, as Lydia was pretending to do now.

Does she realize I am absolute shite at cards?

"Oh am I?" he leered, for the benefit of a passing stranger. This was a role. He was acting.

"Oh, yes." Lydia stroked her fingers down his arm then up again.

Mostly acting.

"Let's start at that table." She pointed and Max followed. To be perfectly honest, he didn't have any better idea than going along with whatever she wanted. If he ended the night empty handed, he was no worse off than when he'd begun.

Well, except for his two pounds six-pence.

Max took a seat at the table she'd directed him to and joined the game. No extra seats were available, so he positioned his chair to allow Lydia to sit on his lap. Neither the dealer nor the other players paid any attention. A handful of other women around the room were doing the same thing, and as far as anyone knew, Lydia was simply one of them.

She sat herself sideways on his lap, wrapping an arm around his neck and pressing her right breast into his chest. Now when he lowered his gaze, he truly could see down her dress. Damn, she had magnificent breasts. Round and plump, with dusky nipples.

Max snapped his attention back to the cards. He lost of course, but Lydia seemed entirely unperturbed. The next round she teasingly ran her fingers over the cards, discreetly pointing out which to play. Hoping she was right, he bet more aggressively than he otherwise might have, and made up the previous loss plus a bit more.

Lydia's hand reached up to caress his cheek. "I knew you would be good."

She was good. Magnificent, in fact. As he played, moving from table to table, she used a series of whispers, taps, and nudges to keep him close to breaking even. And all throughout, he had the extreme pleasure of ogling her breasts and feeling her luscious derriere nestled against his cock. A man could get used to this.

Max splayed his cards on the table, making his fellow players grumble and groan at their loss.

"Can I borrow your girl?" one of the men jested. "She seems to be a good luck charm."

Lydia wrapped both her arms around Max's neck, which thrust her breasts nearly into his face. Good Lord.

"I belong to Maxwell for the night," she said, feigning breathlessness.

If only. His flat wasn't terribly far away. He'd happily give up the cards for a warm bed with a warmer companion.

Lydia slid off his lap, the signal to move on.

Max gathered his chips and rose. "Excuse me, gentlemen."

The other men gave him knowing smirks, then promptly returned to their cards.

Max and Lydia crossed to the other side of the room to continue. As always, Lydia chose the seat, and they slid together into it in a way that now felt entirely natural. The press of her body against his still aroused him, but no longer in an urgent, distracting way. This was not the prelude to a desperate fuck up against a wall, but to a long night of slow and thorough love-making.

It would be good with her. She wasn't merely pretty, but clever and creative, and her nimble fingers felt oh, so good sliding up to tease the little hairs at the nape of his neck.

Max didn't even know the game being played at this table, nor did he care. Lydia was his focus. Even as his body warmed beneath her hands, his eyes kept watch for the cues to follow. Her lips grazed his ear, whispering directions. Her attention, however, was focused elsewhere.

She straightened up, ruffling Max's hair and murmuring nonsense. He followed her gaze to the dealer's hands. Max didn't know enough to learn anything from watching him shuffle and deal, but Lydia surely did. When play began, she watched the man's face. Analyzing.

Max misplayed his hand despite her prompting and lost nearly a third of what he'd won that night. It didn't matter. He understood her strategy now. She was learning the room and how the dealers operated. When she began to look away from the table, Max tracked the movements of her eyes.

His gaze snagged on the fountain. From where they were sitting, it blocked a large portion of the card room, hiding them from the players and dealers on the opposite side of the room.

Max chuckled. "Excellent," he declared, repeating her statement from the day before. It was excellent, indeed. She could win money at one table without anyone across the room noticing. If she moved about strategically, no one would realize how much she was winning until it was too late. And not a soul other than Max had any inkling what she was doing. To everyone else, she was nothing more than part of the scenery.

Impulsively, he kissed her cheek. "You're brilliant."

She let out a sigh of pleasure. "Thank you, darling. Shall we retire after this hand?"

"Yes, I think we shall."

Max lost one final hand, then walked arm-in-arm with Lydia to cash in their chips. Even with his lack of skill, they'd managed a modest profit. He escorted her out the front door and away from prying eyes.

"Do you want your share of the money? We only won because of you."

"Hold on to it. It will be a good amount to begin with tomorrow."

Her voice had resumed its customary crisp tone, without any of the breathy flirtation she'd shown inside. Max's blood went cold. When had he stopped thinking of this night as anything other than a sham?

"I hope you didn't mind any of that, in there," he blurted.

"I'm sorry. I shouldn't have kissed you like that, and I probably shouldn't have been, um…"

"Ogling my tits?" she supplied. One corner of her mouth lifted in a wry smile. "If I was concerned about it, I wouldn't have given you such a view. Don't worry. I'm hardly some innocent chit. I grew up in a club rather like this one."

Grew up in a club? Damned if that didn't make her even more intriguing than she already was. Max gave her a hurried goodnight and set off down the street toward his flat. A cab trundled by, but he didn't hail it. A brisk walk in the cool night air would help him clear his head and remember that her smiles and caresses tonight had been as much a performance as her Madame Xyla act.

"Who are you really, Lydia Weaver?" he asked the empty night.

6
AMMIT
devourer of impure hearts

MAXWELL MILLERSON was unfortunately handsome. At precisely ten p.m. the next night, Lydia found him lounging against the wall outside the Curiosity Club, a pipe in one hand and a book in the other. Utterly charming. Was there any accessory more attractive than a book? Not in her experience.

Even without the book, he cut a fetching figure tonight. The signs of stress had diminished, and a slight smile touched his lips as he read. The nonchalant scholar, in his tidy Harris Tweed suit. He certainly dressed well, for a secretary. Though with an employer like Huntington Black, it may have been a requirement of the position.

Millerson glanced up from his book. Tonight he recognized her at once, despite her change in appearance. She'd opted for a blond wig today, a towering pile of curls secured to her own short hair with what felt like a thousand pins. Her dress, while as revealing as yesterday's, was a far less obtrusive brown wool, adorned with pink ribbon trim.

"Looking for company?" Lydia asked.

Millerson's smile grew to a full grin. He emptied the pipe, tucked it into a pocket, and closed the book. "Not anymore."

He slipped the book into his coat, giving Lydia a glimpse of half the title. *Sense &...* Ah. A man of good taste.

He crooked an arm. "Would you like to accompany me inside?"

Lydia bounced over to take his arm. Today's personality

would be bright and bubbly. "Yes, please. I've never been to a gentlemen's club before. It must be so grand!"

He stifled a laugh. "It aspires to magnificence, certainly. Whether it achieves it is a matter of opinion." His eyebrows arched, making her suspect he was remembering their shared mirth over the absurd decor.

Lydia turned her attention to the club. Best to look at him as little as possible. Relaxed and smiling, he was far too likeable, and she couldn't risk losing her focus. He was a Millerson, and they were her enemies. This was about gaining a connection to the club and putting him in her debt.

They paused at the banker's counter to exchange Millerson's money for tokens.

"I hope you're not intending to win all the money here," he murmured, leaning close to her ear.

Lydia ignored the tingle that ran through her body at the feel of his breath on her skin. "Impossible." The stakes here simply weren't high enough. "But I'll win what I need." Enough to get her invited to play upstairs with the wealthier patrons.

Keeping a silly grin plastered on her face, Lydia bounded across the room to a table she'd selected yesterday as a good starting point. She pulled Millerson along with her, finding him a chair, then plopping down into his lap. When the dealer tossed cards in their direction, she scooped them up.

"Teach me to play, Maxie," she said in a sing-song voice. The other men at the table chuckled.

"Just 'Max,' please," Millerson replied.

Lydia fanned out the cards in front of his face. "What do I do?"

"Uh…"

The other players continued to snicker behind their own cards. Lydia intentionally played poorly, putting them all at ease and losing a small amount of money. When she won the following hand, they smiled and congratulated her. A few more rounds and several pounds in winnings later, the smiles were gone.

She tapped Millerson's foot with hers.

"I think it's time to move on," he declared. Smart man. He'd learned her signals quickly last night and had slipped easily back into his role. Usually her initial readings of people were accurate, but his mind was sharper than she'd realized during their first meeting.

Lydia hopped to her feet and gathered up the chips. "That was fun!" She wasn't even lying. It had been a long time since she'd had an opportunity to use her card skills in this manner. And stunning a group of men who thought her empty-headed made it all the more enjoyable.

They crossed the room to a table on the opposite side of the fountain, then repeated the entire procedure, this time with larger bets. The ruse continued on from there. Max said little, but she could feel his chest shaking with unexpressed laughter every time she shocked another opponent. His body was warm and firm against her back, and she kept expecting the arm he draped casually around her waist to creep down to her thighs or up to her breasts.

Expecting or wanting? she corrected herself. She'd been too long alone, perhaps, if she was considering consorting with a Millerson. Thank goodness she had a goal tonight to distract her from the unwanted lust.

Lydia knew the instant her winning streak turned from an amusement into a concern. Eyes had been on her all night, but the focus of the attention turned to her hands and her face. The dealers were watching her now, not her fellow gamblers. A burly man, who wandered the room looking for any signs of trouble, moved closer. Lydia continued on, unperturbed.

The dealers here weren't skilled enough to necessitate cheating. She'd cut her teeth on gambling tokens and learned mathematics from card-counting and win probabilities. Add in her decade as a spiritualist studying her fellow humans, and she was nigh unstoppable.

She played on, no longer bothering to switch tables. This dealer ran a continual game of Vingt-Un, with men joining and leaving on a regular basis. Lydia knew the odds so well she hardly had to think about her wagers.

Her stack of chips had become a pile. Millerson stashed most of the winnings in his coat pockets, then sat guarding said pockets from anyone nearby.

The dealer made a signal to someone behind Lydia. She didn't bother turning. Her time here was up. She made a quick count of her tokens. Two hundred thirty-four pounds. More than any one person won on an ordinary night at this club, she expected.

"Maxwell."

Lydia did turn now, at the sound of the deep voice speaking Max's name. A tall, thin man with a receding hairline looked down at them, his mouth set in a hard line.

"Father," Max replied coolly. "So good to see you."

Adolphus Millerson. Cold fury clenched around Lydia's heart. The bastard, in the flesh. At last.

She'd never seen Adolphus Millerson before, despite having once pounded on his door every day for two straight months, demanding to speak with him. She'd only stopped when he'd threatened her with incarceration. Perhaps it was because her hatred of him had formed as a teenager, but she'd always imagined he would have a cruel or sinister visage. In truth, he was rather dull. Entirely ordinary, save for the intense bronze eyes that matched his son's.

"Come upstairs, Maxwell," Adolphus said. "And bring your lady friend. I have some friends I'd like her to meet."

Her plan had worked to perfection. Adolphus surely would be hoping to gain back some of the money she'd won here by sending her to play in high-stakes private games. Lydia remembered the setup well from her childhood. Her parents' club had operated in the same way, taking a percentage of the winnings in exchange for furnishing the wealthy patrons with a quiet location, cards, tokens, dealers, if desired, and bouncers to handle any disagreements. Had Millerson directly copied their system? Entirely possible.

Lydia scooped up her chips and popped up from her seat. "I'd love to see the upstairs, Maxie!"

Max rose and offered her his arm. "I'd be happy to show you. Let's exchange your tokens and then I'll walk you up."

"Thank you!" She bounced eagerly as she walked. A good number of people now knew she was a cardsharp, but Lydia intended to retain tonight's chosen personality. A majority of men were distracted by it, whether they wanted to be or not. "This has been so much fun!"

Adolphus trailed close behind them, laughing to himself. "She's a lively one. Didn't think you were the wenching type, boy. Thought you might be a wee bit peculiar, what with all those oddball theater sorts you associate with."

Max stiffened. "I believe we agreed not to discuss my friends."

Lydia turned her head to hide a scowl. Poor Max, having to suffer a cretin of a parent. She reached to pat his arm, catching herself scant inches from touching him.

Stop.

She wasn't supposed to like him. She wasn't supposed to pity him. She had a purpose, and it wasn't to make friends. This club would go down, one way or another.

Lydia bounded up the stairs, feigning enthusiasm. It was time to get to work. Adolphus waved her into the room with the sarcophagus table. The glass tabletop had been removed, replaced with the traditional octagonal baize. Someone must have complained.

"Ooh, a pyramid room!" She giggled. "I love the decor here. So metaphysical! Wouldn't it be a fun place for a seance?"

Adolphus chuckled indulgently. "I'm pleased you like it, young lady."

Lydia surveyed the room's occupants. A club employee sat by the door, a black ledgerbook in his hands. He would be recording all the bets and collecting the club's percentage from any winners when the game broke up. Definitely her parents' system.

Six men sat around the table, all with cards and drinks. None of them looked particularly intent on their game, too busy gesticulating at the walls and discussing the decor. Their conversation halted when they spied the newcomers, and they rose to greet them.

"This the lucky chit you were telling us about, Dolph?" one of them asked.

"Indeed," Adolphus replied. "This is Miss…"

"Marianne Dashwood," Lydia replied. Max would prefer Marianne to Elinor. He had a poetic soul.

His eyebrows rose slightly. Then he gave her an appreciative nod.

"Have a seat, Miss Dashwood," one of the other men offered, pulling out a chair for her. "This will be quite an interesting change, having a lady to cards."

Lydia giggled. "Oh, I'm no lady. But I'm ready to have fun. Already, I have two hundred and thirty four pounds!"

Adolphus gave her a condescending smile. "Much luck to you, my dear. Come, Maxwell, we'd best let them get on with their game."

Max flinched. "Wait… what?"

Lydia looked him straight in the eye, willing him to cooperate. "I'll see you after, Maxie, yes?"

"Of… course," he managed. He inclined his head. "Excuse us. Enjoy the game."

The Millerson men departed, and the door swung closed with a gentle click. Lydia eyed the men around the table, noting their clothing, mannerisms, level of inebriation, and tendency to leer at her.

She would, indeed, be enjoying this. And by the end of the night, step two of her plan would be in motion.

7
MAFDET

protector against venomous animals

Max's FATHER PUSHED ON a section of paneling in the hall, and it swung open to reveal a narrow, dark passageway.

"What the devil?" Max blurted.

"Secret passageway," his father replied. "Discovered it when we did the renovations. Might have been for spying on couples when this was a brothel."

"Not without their knowledge, I hope."

His father waved a hand as if this were irrelevant. "It's my security passage now. We can keep an eye on the games. Watch for cheaters." He put a finger to his lips to signal silence, then pushed Max into the passage ahead of him.

The door swung closed, plunging them into darkness. After a few seconds, Max's eyes adjusted well enough to spy the narrow bands of light high along the corridor wall. Cracks where one could peek into the card rooms, he guessed.

"We opened all the spy holes," his father whispered, nudging Max forward. "Disguised them with those pyramid-stone walls. No one's spotted them yet. Watch your footing, there are little steps beneath each slit."

They'd nearly reached the spy slit that would look into the room where they'd left Lydia. It was a few inches above Max's head, too tall to peer through merely by standing on tiptoe. He approached slowly, sliding his foot along until it contacted the step he'd been warned about. Climbing up onto it brought him exactly eye-level with the spy hole.

"Make sure she doesn't leave until either she's won enough

to earn some money back or someone else has," his father murmured. "And when she's done, escort her out and don't let her back in. No bit of tail is worth this trouble. Keep your lady friends at your own house from now on."

"I can watch her from in the room," Max hissed.

His father huffed. "And risk you getting pulled into their game? We'd lose the club." He turned and walked away, his footsteps barely audible.

You'd lose the club anyway if I hadn't brought her here.

Max contemplated stomping after his father, but concern for Miss Weaver held him in place. She was here to save his arse, and he didn't like leaving her alone in the room with those reprobates. Max didn't know any of the men personally, but he recognized a few of them. They'd also been regulars at some of his father's previous ventures. Nasty sorts, always looking for less-experienced men to take advantage of, and snapping at the waitstaff if their drinks weren't just so.

Thus far, the men were eyeing Lydia with a mixture of amusement and suspicion. They knew she'd been successful downstairs, but weren't yet certain what to make of her. They'd learn soon enough.

She appeared relaxed, her shoulders down and a smile on her face. No doubt she had already learned a thing or two about her opponents. If she was even half as successful as she'd been downstairs, she'd soon be the only one smiling.

And that was why Max couldn't leave. If any of those men began making threats or tried to put his hands on her, Max would be sprinting back up the passageway and coming to her rescue. The man recording the bets was ostensibly a bouncer as well, but Max didn't trust him to be of much use in a crisis. His father had a tendency to keep employee wages low rather than raising them to attract more skilled and loyal staff.

Within minutes, Max's noble purpose was all but forgotten. Lydia Weaver made him believe in magic. She'd picked out the worst of the scoundrels and targeted them, subtly urging them to higher and more reckless bets. Multiple times she bluffed her way to a win.

Eventually, one of the men slammed his cards down on the table. "I've had enough of this bloody draw poker," he snarled.

"It's because you've had too much gin to keep a straight face," another chided. "Vingt-Un?"

The first man huffed an assent.

Poor choice, Max thought.

Lydia had excelled at this game downstairs, where her bets had been so calculated she had to have been counting cards. His father might have called that cheating, but Max thought it was smart play. If you could remember what cards had been played and calculate the odds, why not take advantage of it?

Lydia approved of the new game. Her smile was more genuine now, showing off the entirety of her full bottom lip. When she was faking the smile, her mouth pulled tighter.

And I really shouldn't know that.

Max grimaced. Too much time paying attention to her mouth, apparently. He was a reprobate. Of course he was a reprobate. He was staring at her through a damned secret spy hole.

He shifted from foot-to foot, fighting the temptation to make a noise or poke something through the slit to try to catch her attention. He wanted her to know he was here and ready to help at any moment. But he couldn't risk disturbing her concentration or revealing his presence to the others.

So he watched. And waited.

Lydia's winnings mounted. Any doubts Max had entertained about her ability to win one thousand pounds had long evaporated. Her cards were good and her wagers were better. The men switched games twice more, but nothing helped. Eventually, she gathered up her stack of coins and banknotes and rose from her seat.

"That's enough for me. Thank you, gentlemen."

One of the men stood up and took a menacing step toward her. Max braced himself to run.

"I'm not done with you, you cheating minx," the man growled.

Another man shoved him. "Sod off. She won fair. Let her go."

Lydia took advantage of the argument to scurry over to the bookkeeper and hand him the club's share of her winnings. Max raced down the secret passageway, popping out into the main hall just as she exited the card room. Her eyebrows shot up when she saw him emerge from the wall.

"You were watching?" she guessed.

Max checked that the secret door closed behind him, then joined her. "Yes. I was worried those men might get rough."

"They still could," Lydia replied, moving rapidly toward the stairs. "But I have a knife under my skirts in case of danger."

Well, damn. Now Max was imagining her legs and various ways she may have strapped on a knife. Thank God this was almost over, because he was far too fascinated by this card-playing, fortune-telling, knife-wielding woman.

He walked Lydia out of the building and down the street to the next corner before either of them spoke again.

"One thousand seventy-four pounds in earnings," she announced, pausing to lean against a gas lamp. Reflections of the flickering light danced in her blue eyes, almost seeming to emanate from within. Maybe she *was* magic. She'd done what Max had believed impossible.

Lydia carefully counted out one thousand pounds in bank notes, keeping the money shielded between their bodies to prevent any passers-by from noticing.

"Here you are. As was our bargain." She handed over the money. "I'll be keeping the excess for myself."

She ought to be keeping the whole damned amount for herself. She'd earned it. He'd done nothing but let her into the club.

Lizzie. Think about Lizzie. You can't let her end up on the streets.

Max tucked the money into an inside pocket. He'd be handing it over to the investors first thing in the morning.

"Thank you. Is there anything else I can do for you in return?" He had so little to offer. They wouldn't even allow Lydia back into the club after tonight. His father would be paying close attention to any women visitors from now on.

"Oh, no. I've got what I needed." She flashed a satisfied smile. "I don't think there's another club in the city where I could have done that."

"If you're sure, then," Max said, guilt still eating at him. "If you'd like I could take you to the theater as a thank-you. I could get a backstage tour for *Scarlet and the Wolf.* I know people."

She flinched and gaped at him. "Uh…"

Max had never seen her discomposed before. Shit. He'd done that. Why was he always making a hash of things?

"I'm sorry. That was terribly forward."

Her usual calm snapped back into place. "It was kind of you to offer. But I'm afraid I haven't time for such things at the moment. You kept to our bargain and you owe me nothing more."

Max nodded, afraid to speak and make the situation even more embarrassing.

One side of Lydia's mouth curved slowly upward in a near-smirk. "But do let me know if I can ever be of help again."

She sauntered off into the night, but not before glancing back at him and calling, "Check your pockets!"

Max scrambled to pat down all his pockets, terrified for a few seconds that she'd somehow snatched all the money and run off with it. But, no, the thick wad of banknotes remained exactly where he'd put it. In his left front coat pocket, however, he found a small card with a printed direction to a postal box at the Charing Cross branch of the General Post Office.

Max flipped the card over. In elegant handwritten letters, it read, "Until next time."

8
SESHAT
scribe and record keeper

Since winning the Earl of Bardrick's infamous spiritualist competition two years prior, Lydia had grown accustomed to her position as a comfortably middle-class woman. She had not, however, grown accustomed to taking tea in a mansion in Belgrave Square. Nor did she ever expect to, no matter how many meetings of the Independent Ladies' Suffrage Association she attended.

Lady Virginia Farringdon, daughter of the Earl of Pyne, was the group's leader and founder. Ginny and Lydia had become fast friends, but aside from ILSA, their social circles remained entirely separate. To most ladies of Ginny's acquaintance, Lydia was merely one of those people hired to do things for them. Lydia still spent every day pleased she was now able to hire someone to cook for her.

Despite this disparity, Lord Pyne's butler ushered Lydia into the sumptuous parlor with all the dignity afforded a noblewoman. Tea and sandwiches had been laid out on the sideboard. Lydia helped herself to a cup. The ladies of ILSA did not stand on ceremony during their meetings.

"Goodness, wherever have you been?" Lady Virginia herself swept into the room with her usual exuberant elegance. She poured her own cup of tea, then lowered herself onto an ornate, plum-colored sofa. "You missed last week's meeting and only left us a cryptic note!"

Lydia took a seat beside her friend, once again struck by how very different they were. Ginny's dress was the absolute height of fashion. Layers of pink silk made up her slim skirt, topped by a front-buttoning bodice with narrow pink and burgundy stripes. Lace adorned her cuffs and collar. Her curly black hair had been tied up into neat puffs with matching satin ribbons. If she had used any cosmetics on her dark-brown skin, they were too subtle to notice. Pink gemstones dangled from her ears and around her neck.

Lydia, by contrast, wore a plain dress of green wool, with no trimmings. As usual, she'd painted her lips a soft rose pink, and the only accessory she wore was a pale green turban wrapped over her short hair. Madame Xyla might be fancy, but Lydia was not.

"What was your 'urgent business'?" Ginny prompted. "Was it something terribly exciting? Dangerous? Scandalous?"

"I had to spend most of a day gathering appropriate attire to dress as a lady of the night in order to infiltrate a gentlemen's club and spend a night gambling."

Ginny pulled a small volume from somewhere within the folds of her skirts. "I absolutely must note that down in our list of activities for bold and independent women. I'll put it on the 'less respectable' page. And I'll do it now before Aramina arrives, because you know how horrified she gets at the mere suggestion of anything sexual."

"The prostitute dresses were only for distraction," Lydia argued. "I was playing cards. I wasn't seducing men all night."

But you would have liked to, she reminded herself. *You would have been more than happy to pin bookish Max Millerson to a chair and straddle him.*

"You're turning pink," Ginny observed.

Lydia took an unladylike gulp of tea. "It's warm in here."

Footsteps approached, saving Lydia from further interrogation.

"Miss Aramina Johnson and Lady Constance Blythe," the butler announced. He shut the door as the women scurried into the room to join Lydia and Ginny.

"That's everyone for today," Ginny stated.

"Not quite," Lydia corrected. She set down her teacup and took a folded paper from her reticule. "I have a letter from Tess."

All the other women leaned toward her. "Oh, lovely. Do tell!" Connie exclaimed.

Lydia summarized the letter. "Jack's photography business is booming, so they intend to remain in Boston as their permanent home. They'll continue traveling, of course, to gather information for Tess's guidebooks. But most importantly, they will be coming to London for a visit soon."

Lydia tucked away the letter before she could spend any time looking at the bottom section, where Jack had penned an enthusiastic postscript detailing his excitement over the upcoming visit. The last thing she needed was to grow misty-eyed in front of all her friends.

Lord, how she missed him. They hadn't been apart this long ever before except for those awful years Jack had spent in prison. He was her cousin, but he'd always felt like her twin. Her other half. Adjusting to life without him had been… strange.

"We will make absolutely certain to have Tess come for tea when they are here," Ginny declared. "In fact, we may need to meet more than once in order to hear all the stories of her travels. Today, though, Lydia will entertain us."

Lydia's head snapped around to look at her friend. "Pardon?"

"She had just been telling me about how she gambled at a gentlemen's club the other day," Ginny explained to the others. "Tell us what it was like. Was it a hive of villainy?"

"Not at all. It was an ordinary gaming club except for the decor. The owner has recently redecorated in an Egyptian theme."

"Oh, dear." Aramina sighed. "Why must everyone go so wild for fads these days? I love to learn about ancient civilizations as much as the next person, but we needn't turn our homes into pyramids and steal their artifacts. I don't believe in curses, but, honestly, if I were a mummy I would *want* to put a curse on anyone who tried to grind me up for nonsense cures."

A curse. Lydia's fingers tightened around her teacup. That was it. Her way to bring social ruin on the Curiosity Club and Adolphus Millerson. If enough people believed the club was cursed, haunted, or in any way touched by negative spiritual forces, its downfall would be swift and sure. People loved sensation. Most gamblers believed in luck. Put the two together and it could spell disaster for them. And vengeance for her.

All Lydia needed was a way for Madame Xyla to bring her spiritualist skills into the club. Adolphus Millerson, with his outlandish decor and penchant for fashionable trends, would give her an opening. She only had to prod him in the right direction.

"Ladies," she began. "I have a small favor to ask. Could you casually mention to your acquaintances that you've heard it's now all the rage to hold spiritualist events at gentlemen's clubs?"

Aramina cocked her head to one side. "Are you looking for new business opportunities?" she wondered. "Or is this a plan to admit women to previously forbidden places?"

Lydia sipped her tea. "Why not both?"

And more. Perhaps it was time for Ginny to add "take revenge on one's enemies" to her list.

The next evening, a sultry brunette wafted into the Curiosity Club on the arm of a slightly inebriated gentleman. Once inside, she promptly abandoned him to wander about and bat her eyelashes at other men. She departed alone.

Left in her wake was a scattering of colorful printed cards, bearing the words, "Looking to connect with the realms beyond?" and a contact address for Madame Xyla at the Charing Cross Post Office.

Smoke curled up toward the ceiling, illuminated by the dim glow from the gas lamps overhead. A constant murmur of voices made a smooth, almost musical backdrop to the random clink of glassware. The pub was busy, as usual, full of actors, artists, and the occasional jaded aristocrat yearning for a bohemian lifestyle.

At the bar, a pair of women dressed in masculine attire flirted and laughed. On the sofa across from Max, a young man sat sprawled across another man's lap. This was home. Here in the theater district, Max was free from rules, expectations, and family obligations. Free to be himself.

He crossed out the sentence he'd written and scrawled a new one. Better. Maybe.

Glowering at the mostly blank page, he took another swallow of brandy. He would have preferred absinthe, but he'd been avoiding the club since that night with Miss Weaver. Avoiding her—or her specter—had proven vastly more difficult.

"New play?" Irving Glastonbury flung himself into the next armchair over, blocking most of the light from the nearby lamp.

Irv—whose birth name Max suspected was Tom Smith or something equally mundane—leaned over to see what was on the paper.

"The prince and the fortune teller exchange a heated glance?" Irv raised a single blond eyebrow.

"I was thinking it could be the twist in this story. Instead of falling for the princess, he falls for the fortune teller."

"And what happens to the princess?"

Max shrugged. "She marries someone else? Runs off to be a farmer? It's not important. She's dull. The fortune teller has all the personality."

"People will hate it," Irv predicted.

"That's what you said when I told you I was making the wolf the hero in the last play. But *Scarlet and the Wolf* is my biggest hit yet."

"Fair. Why a fortune teller?"

Because I can't stop thinking about Lydia Weaver and writing is a healthier outlet than most of the alternatives.

Irv must have caught something in Max's expression, because he chuckled and asked, "Inspired by Madame Xyla, were you? I told you she was the answer to all your problems."

"She was the answer to one of my problems," Max replied. "Thank you for the recommendation."

"But the cause of another problem?" Irv scooted his chair closer. "I've seen that look on your face before. You've got a hard-on for the spiritualist, haven't you?"

"No."

Not at the moment.

Irv chortled with laughter. "Good thing you're a writer, Max, and not an actor. You clearly want to tumble her. I take it she's not interested?" He drummed his fingers on the table. "You ought to take up with someone else, then. Get your mind off it. Selena was looking for someone new. And Norm is always up for a romp. Maybe—"

"I don't dally with actors. You know that. Too much conflict if they get—or don't get—a part in my plays."

Irv leaned back in his chair, lacing his hands behind his head and letting out an exaggerated sigh. "I *still* haven't gotten a part in any of your plays, and you dallied with me years ago."

"*Before* I was a playwright."

"And who was that girl? Mary something? She's an actress."

"She didn't start acting until after we'd broken it off." Damn, how long ago was that? Max hadn't had a lover in ages. Maybe it wasn't Miss Weaver. Maybe it was him. He downed the last of his brandy. "I think I'm going home alone tonight, Irv, but thank you."

"Always here to help."

"Always here to stir up drama among the—" Max lost his train of thought when the pub door opened and his father sauntered in. White hot rage flared inside him. "Goddammit."

"Maxwell!" Adolphus Millerson boomed, drawing the attention of everyone in the room. "I'm glad I found you. Had to go to the theater looking for you. They said you might be here."

Max had to set down his pen before he snapped it in half. This was supposed to be his safe space. His refuge. His father had promised years ago to stick to the clubs and leave the theater district to Max.

You know he always lies. Tell him to go to hell.

Max swallowed down the anger. He couldn't do that. The family was relying on him. He'd send his father on his way, firmly but politely.

"I need your help," his father continued.

Max flipped his notebook closed and pocketed both it and his pen. "I don't think this is the place for this sort of conversation."

"Nonsense. I only need a bit of assistance. Not money, this time," he added, before Max could interrupt. "A mummy."

"I beg your pardon?" Max blinked rapidly and looked at his empty brandy glass. How much had he had to drink?

"I've scheduled a mummy unwrapping at the club. Big to-do. Problem is, the mummy I ordered was bad. Crumbled to dust. Hate to say it, but I was scammed. But you'll put it right, won't you? Like your mother always did. I'll need a new mummy by next week. A real one."

Max pushed up out of his chair and faced his father eye-to-eye. "No. Absolutely not. Cancel the event. I am not helping with this nonsense."

"I've sold two hundred tickets."

"Fuck."

"No need to be vulgar, Maxwell. Everything will turn

out fine. You'll make certain of it." He clapped Max on the shoulder. "That's my boy. Have a good night." He spun and strode away without another word.

Max muttered more curses under his breath, then kicked the table so hard that his empty glass flew off and shattered on the floor.

"Sorry. Sorry. I'll pay for that."

"Damn," Irv breathed. "You weren't joking about him. You ought to tell him to go to hell."

The echo of his own thoughts made Max wince. He rubbed his temple against the oncoming headache. "I wish I could. I don't want my sister out on the street."

"Hmm." Irv clapped Max on the back. "You're full of ideas. You'll think of something. And if I hear of anyone with a mummy to spare, I'll let you know."

"Thank you. Maybe tomorrow I can talk some sense into him. I'd better head home now."

"Nah. Sit down. Let me buy you another drink. Leave tomorrow for tomorrow."

Max hesitated a moment. "No. I can't." The pub had lost its sense of comfort, even with his best friend here.

"Very well. But if you need anything—a drink, a fuck, another spiritualist recommendation—you tell me, all right?"

Max gave Irv a weak smile. "All right."

"Good luck."

Max slipped a hand into his pocket and fingered the small rectangle of paper there. He needed more than luck. He needed a professional.

9
KEBECHET

goddess of freshness and
preparation for mummification

LYDIA PULLED ASIDE the curtains to check the weather. Bright and sunny. Perfect. After a full morning giving readings in a darkened room, a long walk outdoors was just what she needed. Perhaps she'd take a hackney to Hyde Park. She had hours until she would need to prepare for this evening's seance.

Her fingers were slipping from the curtain when she spied a man striding toward her door. She froze. Max Millerson. Here? Why? He would have sent word if he'd intended to schedule another card reading. And he hadn't seemed the sort to desire regular spiritual consultation.

Max stopped abruptly several yards from her front door, shook his head, then turned around. He walked away, paused, walked back. Pacing. Now and then, he lifted a hand to his temple, rubbing as if he had a headache.

The anxiety she'd witnessed when she'd first met him had returned. Another problem with the club? But if that were the case, wouldn't he have sent a message to the address she'd provided him?

Lydia jerked and dropped the curtain. Maybe he had. She hadn't been to the post office in a few days. If his problem was urgent, he might have decided to come directly to her.

"Which means he knows who I am."

A shiver raced down her spine. She didn't actively strive to keep her identity as Madame Xyla a secret. People in the neighborhood knew who she was, as did her friends. Clients were uninterested in her real name. Most people saw only what they wanted to see.

Lydia snatched the gold robe she'd left draped over the back of her chair and wrapped it around her simple lavender dress. On her way to the door, she glanced at the hall mirror to check her turban, tucking in a few stray wisps of blond. The headpiece wasn't adorned like the ones she usually wore as Madame Xyla, but it wouldn't stand out as unusual if Millerson expected the spiritualist.

She pulled open the door. "Can I help you?"

He jumped. "Miss Weaver!"

Lydia fought to keep her expression impassive, though that shiver of unease once again ran through her. He did know her identity. Probably had from the beginning. Which meant even through his worry and the spectacle of the card reading, he'd seen her. Seen *Lydia*.

"Excuse me. Madame Xyla." Max strode toward the door. "Forgive me for intruding."

Lydia waved him inside. "You appear troubled, Mr. Millerson. Another problem with the club?"

"Yes, of a sort." He stepped through the door and removed his hat, but didn't continue any further. "I probably shouldn't have come here, but once again I find myself with nowhere else to turn." His fingers dug into the felt of his hat brim. "Please don't hesitate to send me packing, if I'm imposing on you."

Lydia removed the gold robe and hung it on a peg on the wall. "Let's refrain from any pretensions, shall we? You know who I am, and your problem is not of a spiritual nature."

"No," he admitted. "And yes, I've always known who you were. When you declined to inform me that Miss Weaver and Madame Xyla were one and the same, I assumed you preferred to keep your two lives separate. I apologize for taking advantage of my knowledge in coming here." He didn't glance away, but looked boldly at her, prepared to accept any censure she might bestow.

Lydia accepted the apology with a slight nod. "You have a pressing issue, or you wouldn't have come directly here, and I did leave you with an offer of future assistance. It seems we need only discuss the problem and how we might help one another. Why don't we step outside and walk a while? It may settle your nerves."

"Er, yes." He glanced down at his hat, realized the damage he was inflicting on it, and placed it back on his head. "That's a fine idea. It's a lovely day."

"Quite."

They stepped outside and Lydia closed and locked the door behind her.

"I promise not to take too much of your time," Max said. "I need to return to work before long."

Lydia took his arm and started down the street. "Let's not dally, then. Tell me what this new trouble is. Another financial crisis?"

"Not quite." He hesitated a moment, then laughed. "It's ridiculous, honestly. Now that I'm talking about it, it seems the most absurd of things. My father needs a mummy."

"A mummy? Doesn't he have several of those already?"

"A real mummy. He plans to hold an unwrapping event."

Lydia grimaced. This was not the sort of event she'd been hoping for. Trust Adolphus Millerson to muck everything up. She would have to make do.

"Would you like me to speak with him as Madame Xyla? I'd be happy to contact the spirit of this mummy, who will no doubt profess that he would like to be left in peace, thank you very much."

"I'd love to see such a performance." Max's lips quirked upward into a half-smile, which faded as quickly as it had formed. "Unfortunately, he has already sold tickets to this event, and probably spent all the money he earned from those sales. I know it's silly to hope you might have any idea of how to help. I don't even want to help, to be honest. I think desecrating mummies is a revolting practice. And I have very little to offer you, at any rate. I haven't any spare cash, and my father has banned all women from participating in gaming at the club. Unless you would like me to introduce you to some of my theater friends? I know costumers and prop makers who might have useful items for your spiritualist act."

Lydia almost stumbled. Yes, on the surface, his offer was a paltry one. But never in her decade as Madame Xyla had anyone given her help or suggestions. Everything she owned, she'd bought herself. Everything she did, she'd learned on her own. She was competent, independent. She didn't need help. And here was her enemy's son casually offering it.

He mistook her silence for disinterest. "I know. Your assistance is worth so much more than that."

"No, I think it's a fair price," Lydia countered. "Anyone who deals with people the way I do must regularly hone their craft. And it's been too long since I've added anything new to my repertoire. The theater is exactly what I need. I always want my readings and seances to be engaging and entertaining. Those are the things that set me apart from other spiritualists and encourage people to return for more."

"Oh!" Max's entire face brightened. His smile smoothed out the worried creases in his brow and made his copper-brown eyes twinkle. He absolutely needed to smile more often.

At anyone other than Lydia. That smile was far too potent, and she didn't need to be distracted from her goals. A mummy unwrapping wasn't quite what she'd had in mind, but she could utilize it for her purposes. She needed to seize this opportunity. She looked away from Max's distracting gaze, making a pretense of avoiding a man walking in the opposite direction.

"I can't take you to the theater today," Max went on. "I have work to do this afternoon." He pulled a face and his eyes flicked briefly skyward. "But tomorrow is Sunday and I'll be available all day."

So would she. "You won't be spending the day in a church repenting of your sinful ways?" she teased.

"I like my sinful ways."

Honest. Some people might think him impudent, but Lydia appreciated his bluntness. "That makes two of us," she replied. "Tomorrow it is. Now, let's return to this mummy problem of yours. We don't want to use a real mummy, but we want one that appears real. Can't your prop-maker friends create something?"

Max steered her around the corner, waited for a carriage to rattle past, then escorted her across the street. "They can certainly make wrappings that appear old, as long as the mummy doesn't need to pass expert inspection. It's the insides that concern me, however. Where does one find a false desiccated corpse? I'm a bit afraid to ask any of my friends. They might suggest we simply rob a grave."

Lydia arched an eyebrow. "You have interesting friends."

"I do. And many of them say outrageous things. I'm never certain which of those things are true and which aren't."

The same could be said of speaking to a spiritualist. Perhaps this was why he didn't seem to make the same distinction between Madame Xyla and Lydia Weaver that the rest of the world did.

"Let me handle the inside of the mummy," she said. "I know interesting people too." People with the skills to create a spectacle that would give the viewers their money's worth. And more.

Max grinned at her. "I think we have the beginning of a plan. You are a marvel, Lydia Weaver. Is that where your name comes from? Weaving intangible threads into something real?"

She didn't want to smile back at him. She truly didn't. Her mouth simply moved of its own accord. "I think my ancestors made cloth. I assume yours ran a mill?"

"Oh, no. I'm descended from a great warrior who was called 'The Miller' because he ground his enemies to dust."

Lydia's smile widened. "Is that so?"

"Absolutely. At least, it's what I've always told myself. I've never spoken with my ancestors, not being a spiritualist."

"Perhaps you'll have to come by for another session some day."

Lydia forced herself to look away again. Good God, she was flirting. Not fake flirting like she'd done at the club, but genuine, lure-this-man-to-my-bed flirting. She never flirted. Damn him for being so likable.

"I would enjoy that," Max replied. He reached into his pocket and withdrew a silver pocketwatch, flipping open the lid. "I ought to be going. I have a great deal of work still to do today. But I will come by your house tomorrow and escort you to the theater. Is one p.m. acceptable?"

Lydia nodded. "That will do nicely. Thank you."

Max bid her adieu, and they parted, he heading off toward Trafalgar Square, while she turned back toward Covent Garden. Hyde Park could wait for another day. Today, Lydia had a curse to conjure up.

10
PTAH
god of architects and craftsmen

The Enchantment Theatre in the Haymarket district had been Max's favorite place in the world since he'd attended its opening performance more than eight years prior. The short-lived show had been a comedic interpretation of Beauty and the Beast. Max didn't remember much of it. But he did remember staring at the neoclassical facade adorned with colorful playbills and thinking he'd found a home.

The same feeling enveloped him as he approached the now-familiar building with Miss Weaver at his side. He grinned at the bright red and yellow playbill that boldly advertised his own work. On a Sunday afternoon, the area was quiet, but in the evenings the whole street glowed with the dancing light of the gas lamps and rang with the happy chatter of theatergoers.

"This is where we would enter for a performance," Max said with a wave of his hand. "But today we'll use the rear entrance. I have a key."

"Excellent. I've been through the front entrance, though not when the theater is empty. But I've never seen backstage before." Lydia Weaver wasn't one to bounce, unless she was playing a role, but there was a definite spring in her step as she followed him around the side of the building.

Max had to quash the urge to spin her into a dance in the middle of the street. She was genuinely delighted to be here. His meager offering truly meant something to her. A sizzle of excitement flowed through his veins at the thought that she might feel something akin to what he did when coming here.

She would fit in with his friends. She would take an interest in his work.

"You're a theatergoer?" he asked, to prevent his imagination running away. Theirs was still a business relationship, not a friendly one.

"I am," she replied. "I enjoy performances of many varieties. The theater offers many of the same things spiritualism does: entertainment, spectacle, and a way to remove oneself for a time from the mundanity and gloom of the real world. I suppose we are like cousins." A slight wistfulness came into her eyes at this last sentence.

"I like that way of thinking about it." Max unlocked the door and held it open for her. "Here we are."

Light from a row of gas lights filled the back corridor. It meant someone else was here, which didn't surprise Max. He couldn't remember a time he'd found the building completely deserted. Most importantly, it meant he didn't have to go about lighting lamps so they could see.

"We're in the main backstage hall now," he said. "The rooms all along the right side are the dressing rooms. Feel free to take a peek inside if you like. They're all much the same. Dressing tables and mirrors and some racks of costumes."

An echoing, muffled voice came from off to their left, beyond the doors leading to the stage.

"The stage is through there?" Lydia inquired.

"Yes. It sounds as though someone is rehearsing. We'll go there later. Let me take you down to the trap room first."

Max led the way to the stairs and peered down into the darkness. The lamps below-stage had, unfortunately, not yet been lit. He dug into his pockets for a box of matches, then headed down. He struck a match, opened the valve on the nearest lamp, and lit it. The warm glow illuminated perhaps a third of the room well enough to see. Max lit a few more lamps in strategic locations while Lydia began to explore.

"These are pretty," she remarked, fingering some colorful

dresses hanging in the costume corner. "Is there a production here set during the Regency?"

"Those were from the play that ran prior to *Scarlet and the Wolf*," Max explained. "A Napoleonic melodrama. The women all wore those, and the men wore red coats."

Now he was imagining Lydia wearing one of those dresses. She would be a sight to behold, with an empire waist and low neckline displaying her generous bosom.

"I've always enjoyed clothing from other time periods," Lydia continued. "My cousin is a photographer, and I've dressed up to model for him at times." A hint of a smirk played on her face. "You may have seen me as someone's ghostly ancestor."

Her comment distracted Max—somewhat—from his daydreaming. "Are you, as a spiritualist, telling me spirit photographs are a hoax?"

She sniffed. "Everyone knows spirit photographs are a hoax. I leave that nonsense to Jack." She stepped away from the costumes. "What other interesting things do you have down here?"

"Props of all varieties," he replied, making a sweeping gesture with one hand. "Some are real things the theater has collected over the years, others are made of painted wood, plaster, and other inexpensive materials. If you see anything that might be useful for your work, we can set it aside. Anything you aren't able to borrow can probably be replicated for a reasonable price."

Lydia picked up a lantern and studied it for a moment before setting it back down. "I'm interested in the lighting. I've seen the way lights are used in theatrical productions, but it's something I've never employed in my own work. Now that I own my own house, however, it becomes a possibility."

Max nodded toward the stairs. "You'll want to see the stage, then. That's where all the lights and controls are." Thudding footsteps overhead made him look up. "Assuming whoever's emoting up there finishes someday."

Lydia chuckled and continued her perusal of the space. "Are the swords real?" She drew a saber from a rack of weapons. Adopting something resembling a fighting stance, she pointed the sword at his chest. "Your time is up, Millerson. Surrender now, or die by my blade."

Well, well, well. Cool and sensible Miss Weaver had a playful side. Max couldn't be too surprised, given the enthusiasm with which she'd thrown herself into her gambling courtesan persona. He hadn't expected to witness this side of her, however.

"Surrender? Hah!" He grabbed a sword from the rack. "You have sealed your own fate, vile fiend, for I am a swordsman of great renown!" Or a regular practitioner of stage fighting, but that didn't have nearly as nice a ring to it.

Lydia swatted at his sword. The clang of metal-on-metal reverberated through the room. Max retreated, taking up a defensive stance, and focusing on her movements. She looked to have little to no training, which meant he didn't know what she might do. And while he suspected he could disarm her with a few quick moves, that would end the fun when it had barely begun. Better to feel her out.

She attacked methodically, trying different angles each time. Max parried every one, letting himself sink into the sensations of flexing muscles and clashing swords. His feet moved in practiced steps. He couldn't tell a waltz from a quadrille, but he had this dance memorized.

"You're good at this," Lydia applauded, when he countered yet another thrust, sending her skittering backward to avoid his blade.

"I told you. I'm descended from a great warrior."

Their swords crashed together. Max spun away from the blow in a move that would likely have gotten him skewered on a battlefield, but looked great on the stage. He drove Lydia back, then relented and let her retake the offensive.

"What the devil is going on down there?" an irritable voice intruded from above.

Max faltered, missed a block, and took a hit to his arm. "Ow!" He looked up. A scowling face outlined with bushy whiskers peered down from the open trap door. "Haskins. Hello."

"This isn't your personal play place, boy," Haskins growled. "Go woo your doxy somewhere else."

Lydia walked over to the trap door and stared straight up. "I am no doxy, sir, and I thank you not to insult women in so cavalier a manner."

Haskins huffed. "Typical of you to find a saucy one with big words. Off with you both. Some of us are working here." He vanished from the opening and the trap door banged closed.

"I apologize for him." Max slotted his sword back into the rack. "Haskins is perpetually grumpy because he's always cast as the grizzled old man, and he thinks he should play Hamlet. We keep telling him to try shaving off that bushy beard, but he won't have it."

Lydia returned her own sword to its place. "He plays the villain in *Scarlet and the Wolf*, doesn't he?"

Max started. She'd seen his play? Butterflies fluttered in his stomach.

Please tell me you didn't hate it.

"Yes," Max replied. He stuffed his hands in his pockets to keep from fidgeting. "He does a fabulous job, too. He's an excellent actor, grumpiness aside."

Lydia's grin made her whole face seem to glow. "I adored that play."

Max had to turn away from her gaze. Adoring his play was possibly even worse than hating it would have been. Because now he wanted to hug her, and already they'd gone past the bounds of their business arrangement.

"Is there anything else you'd like to examine before we leave this room?" he asked hurriedly. "I'll show you the stage as soon as Haskins finishes. He can't monologue forever."

"Are you certain about that?" Lydia laughed softly and turned to look inside a nearby chest of drawers.

Max bit his lip and said nothing. He couldn't trust himself not to say the wrong thing. For the next quarter hour he hovered silently behind her as she poked into every box and corner. She loved his play! Part of him wanted to beg her to talk all about it and ask him every question she could think of. But he couldn't do that. He'd neglected to tell her that he was the playwright when she'd brought up the subject. Now it would be awkward. Wouldn't it?

And he used a pen name for a reason. Only the people at the theater knew his identity. If his father ever found out, he'd find some way to exploit it.

Max shuddered. *Never.*

Lydia straightened up from the box she was examining. "I don't hear anything from the stage anymore."

Max paused to listen. Silence. "Capital." He hurried to the nearest lamp and turned off the gas. "Let's go."

He didn't quite rush her up the stairs and to the stage, but he didn't linger, either. Best to focus on his real reason for being here. She got ideas for her business, he got a mummy. Nothing further.

After a quick look at the backstage props and sets for *Scarlet and the Wolf,* Max led Lydia to the prompt side of the stage, just out of sight of the audience.

"This is the gas table," he said. He indicated a wooden table with an upright board behind. Dozens of valves jutted from the apparatus, painted in various colors and labeled with words meaningless to the uninitiated. "This is where all the lighting magic happens."

Lydia ran her fingers over the smooth wood, then touched a valve. "Show me how it works."

"These valves control every light in the house. The gas pipes all run to this table, where the valves can be opened and closed to regulate the flow of gas. This row here at the top is for the house lights." Max twisted several valves to dim them. "Now only the stage is illuminated."

Lydia peeked out at the theater. "Fascinating. And the rest are for the stage?"

"Exactly. Footlights here, border lights here. They're turned up and down as the scene dictates. Several of these are spot lighting for particular locations."

"How do you control the mood of the lighting? The color and that sort of thing?" she wondered. "The lights were used so well in *Scarlet and the Wolf.* Especially in the moonlit scene. The romantic atmosphere added a great deal to the impact, I thought. You've seen the play, I assume?"

"Many times." Dammit, they were back to talking about his play. And now it would be beyond awkward and into embarrassing if he brought up his role in the production.

"Show me how you make the moonlight," Lydia prompted. "I want to be able to create that sort of ethereal illumination in my seance room."

Max cleared his throat. *Keep to the bargain.* "We have a series of colored lights. What you see now on stage is what we would use for day lighting. For night scenes, we turn those down, and turn other lights up. I can take you out on the stage to point them out, but they're covered with glass or cloth filters of different colors. Some we can rotate to alter the colors, but right now they're all purples and blues." Max made the adjustments. "See? Now it's night."

Lydia walked out onto the stage, spinning in a slow circle to take in the entire space. Max's breath hitched. She belonged here, in this fantasy of moon and stars. She kept herself aloof, guarded from the world, but today he'd had a glimpse of who she was when let free.

"You could have been an actress," he observed. "You look natural on the stage." He turned the moon spotlight on, casting a pool of soft blue light at her feet.

"It's the lighting." She tipped her face up to the moonlight. "It's so beautiful."

Max crossed the stage to her side. "I was thinking the same thing."

"I'm not even a romantic sort, and I can feel something of how the actors must feel during a performance."

For once, the astute Miss Weaver had misread someone. She had romance in her blood, even if she kept a tight rein on it.

"Thank you for bringing me here," Lydia continued. "Not only am I inspired to improve my seance room, but it's a pleasure to see the secrets behind one of my all-time favorite plays."

Max gaped. An all-time favorite? Bollocks. He needed to say something. How did one tactfully say, "Funny story. Actually, I'm the author of said play"?

"It was all so cleverly done," Lydia went on, before Max could come up with a solution to his predicament. "I particularly liked how the references to the original fairy tale were framed so the audience would recognize them, even when Scarlet never used the word 'grandmother' or said any of the iconic lines. Not until the very end, which I loved." She gazed out at the scattered dots of starlight covering the stage floor. She waved a hand out at the seating area. "First, Scarlet startled the entire audience when she said, 'I think we make a damned fine team.' It was delightful. But Wolf wasn't startled. Or shocked, or repelled. He simply gazed at her adoringly, right here in the moonlight. And then he said—" She turned back to Max and froze, her lips parting, and her gaze locking on his mouth.

His heartbeat counted out several silent seconds. "Why, Scarlet," he breathed, "what a lovely mouth you have." He listed toward her. When had they gotten so damned close? He could feel her exhalations and see the sheen of moisture on her lips, sparkling beneath the silvery moon.

She rose up on tiptoe, leaning closer, closer.

The stage lights flared up into their full sunlight glory. Max and Lydia sprang apart.

"Who turned out all my lights?" a trilling soprano voice complained. "No respect for my gas table. They'll be setting this place on fire one day, mark my word."

Max took two more steps away from Lydia. "Mrs. Pugh. Beg pardon." The words came out in a rush. "I was demonstrating the lighting system for a friend. She's interested in installing a similar setup in her home. I'm sure she would love to benefit from your expertise."

Lydia had broken free from whatever enchantment had caused her to nearly kiss him. She stood straight-backed and stoic, and when she spoke her words were cool and even.

"Yes, I would like that. Mrs. Pugh, is it? May I contact you here at the theater if I have questions?"

Mrs. Pugh frowned at Lydia for a moment, then shrugged. "If you'd like. Though I don't see why a proper lady like yourself needs theater lighting."

Lydia gave her a friendly smile. "It's a business investment. Thank you. I ought to be going now. Please excuse us."

Max walked Lydia out to the street, where she hailed a passing cab. "Until next time," he said, handing her up into the vehicle.

She nodded. "I will be in contact once I've seen to my half of the bargain." The door swung closed, and the cab rolled away.

Max blew out a long breath. He hadn't entirely scared her away, thank God. He'd definitely overstepped, however. It was inevitable, he supposed, taking her into a place of magic and fantasy. From now on, private encounters in the moonlight would be off limits.

11
BASTET

protector of the home, goddess of childbirth and cats

"YOU CAN PUT THE MUMMY in the seance room," Lydia instructed. She motioned to the open door. The two burly men in tidy matching suits carried the long wooden box into the room, placing it on the floor near the seance table. One of them withdrew a paper from his coat pocket.

"Himself left you instructions." He passed the paper to Lydia. "Enjoy communing with the dead." Both the men tipped their hats, then departed.

Lydia hitched up her skirts and sat cross-legged on the floor beside the box. Her Madame Xyla clothing was well-suited to activity of this sort. The flowing skirts and petticoats fluffed up around her, allowing her to settle into whatever position she desired. Her everyday dresses would never have worked for this, though she did specially alter her clothing for more freedom of movement than the slim, tight style of the day usually permitted.

The top of the box—or coffin, she supposed—lifted off easily. Lydia pushed it aside and surveyed the mummy within. The bandages supplied by Max's theater friends looked the part. The fabric was worn and frayed, dry and brittle to the touch, and colored to appear brown with age. The outside would serve its purpose. She could only trust that the inside would do the same.

Lydia unfolded her letter.

Treat with care. Bones are plaster replicas from a medical institution and apt to breakage. Gold jewelry woven into bandages as requested. Authenticity uncertain, as they were liberated from a collector. Torso contains surprise sure to cause a spectacle. Will not harm unwrapper or viewers. Cut carefully and slowly with sharp knife. Diagram of placement of artifacts and where to make incisions is below. I await news of results.

-C

The diagram had been crafted with care, the proportions exactly matching those of the real mummy. Julian Carter had certainly come through for her.

Lydia grimaced. She owed him now, and this favor was far bigger than her request for a street swindler. But no matter. She would think of a way to pay him back. She always did. It was too bad he preferred favors to cash. These days she had the money to pay.

Lydia tucked the letter into one of the spacious pockets in her skirt, then rose to her feet, leaving the coffin open. Max Millerson would be arriving soon to see the mummy and discuss details for the unwrapping event. Hopefully he'd made arrangements for her to attend. She needed to be present to ensure everything went according to plan and to prepare for the aftermath.

Her one remaining issue was finding someone to pose as an archaeologist. The unwrapping needed to be conducted according to the instructions Carter had left. She might need to pay someone from the theater for a night's performance.

A shrill whistle announced an arrival at her front door. The fancy compressed-air doorbell didn't make the most pleasant of sounds, but Lydia loved it regardless. Its modern technology marked her as a woman of the scientific age, just as her newly-planned adjustable gas lighting would.

She scurried to the door and pulled it open. "Good afternoon, M—" She faltered at the sight of a pair of dazzling blue eyes with a partial heterochromia. "Jack! My God, Jack!

You're here!" Lydia launched herself at her cousin, who caught her in a fierce embrace. "Why didn't you send word you'd arrived in England?"

"Surprise!" he teased.

Lydia thumped him on the back. "Bastard." The word came out slightly choked. Tears welled in the corners of her eyes. He was here. Finally. He was here and her heart was whole.

"Missed you, too," Jack said, kissing her cheek before releasing her. He gave her a lopsided grin. "Who knew all it took to get you to express your emotions was for me to run off for a while?"

Jack's eyes were misty too, but that was typical. He'd always worn his heart on his sleeve. So, naturally, her response to his ribbing was to resume her usual stoicism.

"Come inside," she instructed. She looked past Jack to the woman who stood behind him, in a sensible traveling dress and holding a squirming infant. "I need to greet Tess properly and meet my niece, and that's better done indoors." A ball of black fur streaked past her legs and vanished into the house. "And we need to retrieve your ghost cat."

She ushered the group inside. Jack hung his hat on a peg, then began peering through each doorway in turn. "Look at this house. You're a high-class lady now! Too good for a scoundrel like me."

"Jack, our house in Boston is as big as this one," Tess pointed out. "Complete with a fancy photo studio."

"I know. Too good for the likes of me."

Lydia couldn't hold back a smile at the pride coloring his voice. She was proud too. They'd done this, the two of them. Scraped their way up to a secure, comfortable life. Together. God, how she loved him.

To avoid coming over all mawkish, Lydia turned to Tess. Her cousin-in-law would be a comfortable conversationalist.

And give real answers to Lydia's questions instead of flippant ones.

"You're well then?"

"Very," Tess answered. "Happy and thriving." Tess beamed down at the little girl in her arms, and Lydia's vision blurred again.

Dammit.

"We must have dinner together tonight," Lyda declared. By evening her emotions would be settled again and they could talk properly. "I want to hear everything. Now, let me meet this new little Weaver."

Tess handed over the baby. "Alexandria, meet your Aunt Lydia."

Lydia bounced the baby, smiling down into her chubby face. "Hello, little Alex."

Alexandria was a perfect cherub. Her sparkling eyes were Weaver family blue, with the hereditary brown patch. Tufts of auburn hair matched her mother's curls. Lydia gave the baby a squeeze. Love at first sight was real.

"Ga!" Alexandria exclaimed, reaching for the embroidered flowers adorning Lydia's turban.

"You like it? I'll find one for you to play with. And when you're bigger I will teach you all my fun tricks."

A few tears escaped at last and trickled down Lydia's cheek. She surrendered to the love welling up inside her. It was beautiful, and if it overwhelmed her, so be it.

Family.

Family had always meant everything to her. She had adored her parents and her aunt and uncle. After she'd lost them, Jack had been her entire world. He'd left home for a new beginning, but he hadn't left Lydia alone. Instead, he'd expanded their family by marrying Tess. Now he'd added a mischievous toddler to spoil and adore.

"My family," Lydia murmured. "Even across an ocean, you'll always be mine."

"Bloody hell!"

Lydia flinched and spun around. Jack had disappeared into the seance room.

"Why the devil do you have a mummy in your parlor?" he called.

"A mummy?" Tess hurried after. As an author and journalist, she was never one to miss a good story.

Lydia followed, the baby still in her arms. "This is my seance room, as you ought to be able to tell from the decor. I converted the parlor because it's closest to the entrance. Easy access for my clients. The rest of the house is my personal space."

Jack stood above the mummy, arms folded across his chest. "But why a mummy? Ghastly thing. It doesn't seem your style."

"It's a fake."

"Thank God."

Tess joined her husband beside the coffin. "Whyever do you have it? I know everything Egyptian is popular, but people don't want to… talk to mummies, do they?"

"It's not for my act. It's for an event. I was asked to provide a fake mummy for an unwrapping."

Jack raised an eyebrow. "And you agreed? Why?"

Lydia had no choice but to explain. Especially because Jack was the perfect answer to her archaeologist conundrum. He was a practiced conman. He would put on a good show.

"This mummy is special. It's designed to create a spectacle that will convince the audience they have invoked the mummy's wrath and brought a curse upon the venue."

"A curse?" An impish grin spread across Jack's face. "Why, Lydia Weaver, are you embroiled in a wild scheme? And I thought you were the sensible one."

Lydia put on her "sweet and innocent" smile. It was her turn to tease. "You weren't here to beg me to join one of your ridiculous swindles, so I had to do it myself. But now that you *are* here..." She let the sentence trail off, knowing it would make her cousin squirm.

"What?" Jack demanded.

"I need you to be my archaeologist. Attend the unwrapping with me and open up the mummy according to these instructions." Lydia shifted Alexandria to one hip and retrieved the letter from her pocket.

Jack read the missive. "Who's 'C'? Not Julian Carter, I hope? Lydia, that man is a menace."

She shrugged. "He's always been nice to me."

For a man who spent most of his time smiling, Jack had a surprisingly effective scowl. "He acts as if he's Robin Bloody Hood, and yet all the money he steals mysteriously vanishes. He probably owns a small island with mountains of treasure."

Lydia couldn't declare such a statement entirely impossible. Julian Carter was a thief and a scoundrel. He had a host of disreputable acquaintances. Still, he wasn't a bad sort.

She waved a hand toward the hall. "You'd best be going, if you think I shouldn't consort with charming rogues."

As if she had summoned it forth, the doorbell whistled.

Jack startled. "Was that some new spiritualist gimmick?"

"The doorbell," Lydia replied. "Excuse me. I'm expecting someone."

"Are we interrupting?" Tess asked. "We can leave if you need us out of the way. Although I suppose we ought to find Phantom first."

Lydia had no doubt the little black cat had found herself a cozy piece of furniture to curl up on. No sense disturbing her. Lydia wasn't letting her family leave any time soon.

"You're not interrupting," she replied. "This is about the mummy, so Jack should be a part of it."

"When did I agree to participate?" Jack complained, though the entire room knew the words were a sham. He loved intrigue.

Lydia hurried to the front door, still carrying the baby.

Alex had gotten a good grip on Lydia's turban and tugged it loose. Lydia pulled it off and let her have it. She had plenty more up in her bedroom.

Max Millerson waited on the front stoop, dressed in his usual scholarly style. Lydia hadn't seen him since that day at the theater, and somehow she'd forgotten how very handsome he was. Or perhaps she'd only been trying not to think about it. She'd been far too close to kissing him.

She'd been caught up in the moment, that was all. It had been ages since she'd had a day where she'd simply had fun. Years, perhaps. That, combined with the magic of the stage lighting, had addled her senses. It wouldn't happen again. She had nothing to fear from a pretty face or an affectionate smile.

She looked him straight in the eye when she said, "Hello, Max."

"Hello."

He looked especially well today, smiling and almost as relaxed as he'd been at the theater. No worries about the mummy unwrapping, then. He trusted her to keep her end of the bargain.

A pang of guilt stabbed at her, but she shoved it away. This wasn't about him, and she'd been true to her word. She'd acquired a mummy for him.

"Have you become a mother since I saw you last?" Max wondered, indicating Alexandria.

"My niece," Lydia explained. "Technically my cousin, I suppose, but since Jack is as good as a brother, she feels like a niece. Please, come inside."

Max followed her through the door and into the seance room, where Jack and Tess still stood by the mummy, quietly talking. They paused when Lydia entered.

"Jack, Tess, allow me to introduce Mr. Maxwell Millerson. Mr. Millerson, this is my cousin, Jack Weaver, and his wife Tess. They are the parents of Alexandria here." Lydia set the child down. Alex took two wobbly steps before falling and crawling the rest of the way to her parents, dragging Lydia's turban along with her.

"A pleasure to meet you, Mr. Millerson," Tess said.

Jack simply nodded.

"The mummy is right over here, if you'd like to see it," Lydia said to Max. "I'm pleased to tell you that Jack will be our archaeological expert for the night and will conduct the unwrapping in proper scientific fashion."

A furrow appeared in Max's brow. "I thought you said your cousin was a spirit photographer."

Jack flashed a charming smile. "I am a man of many talents."

Max considered this for a moment. "An actor? Or a confidence man?"

Jack's laugh rang throughout the room. "I like you already, Millerson. How did you come to be a part of this bizarre affair?"

Lydia's mouth twisted, stuck somewhere between a smile and a frown. Was it good or bad that Jack and Max had become instantly friendly? Though perhaps it was inevitable. Max was endlessly likeable.

"It's my father who wants the mummy," he explained. "The unwrapping will be held at his club."

"Ah. So you hired Lydia to give you a show?" Jack nodded thoughtfully. "Good idea. People always love her performances."

"Miss Weaver is a woman of many talents," Max stated, with such conviction that Lydia's heart skipped a beat. "It must be a family trait."

"You're very kind, Mr. Millerson," she replied.

She spoke the absolute truth. Max was a good man. He had admired and respected her abilities from the day they'd met. He was pleasant to everyone, even the grumpy man who'd yelled at them at the theater. And he was entirely too charitable to his unworthy bastard of a father.

That unwelcome pang of guilt returned, and again she refused to dwell on it. She had a mission.

Max knelt beside the mummy. "This looks perfect." He glanced up at Lydia. "I could almost believe it was real."

"I am eighty-five percent certain it uses no human remains."

"Eighty-five percent?"

"The man who helped build it is not entirely trustworthy."

"Well." Max rose to his feet, brushing his trousers clean of any fuzzy particles Lydia's plush carpet may have left behind. "I suppose it's the best we can do. Thank you, again, Miss Weaver. Would you like me to arrange transportation of the artifact to the club, or do you prefer to do it yourself?"

"Jack and I will bring it with us. I *am* invited, correct?"

Max gave her a dazzling smile. "Of course! I wouldn't dream of holding this event without you. Even if my father objected, I'd find a way to sneak you in. Hide you in the secret passage, if necessary. But he won't object. Having both an archaeologist and a spiritualist will give the event an aura of authenticity."

She returned his smile. Her plans were progressing. "Excellent. Two days from now, at eight p.m.?"

Max nodded. "Best to arrive by seven to leave plenty of time to prepare."

"Seven it is," Lydia agreed.

"Capital. I will let you return to your family now." He gave her a slight bow. "I can see myself out. Good day, Miss Weaver."

"Good day, Mr. Millerson."

The moment the front door rattled closed, Jack turned to her, a devilish grin on his face. "Someone's been having fun since we've been gone."

Lydia busied herself putting the top back on the mummy's coffin. "I have no idea what you mean."

"No need to be coy, darling. Have you been seducing all the handsome men, or merely the one?"

"I don't think the seduction is complete," Tess observed. "There was far too much longing in his gaze."

Jack slid close to Tess and put an arm around her waist. "Perhaps the longing is for a repeat seduction," he murmured.

Lydia scowled at her cousin. "I do not want to watch you two canoodling."

"You're right, love," Jack said to Tess. "Incomplete seduction. Lydia is much too frustrated. We'd best be on our way so she can get on with chasing him down."

"Mr. Millerson and I have a business arrangement and nothing more," Lydia stated firmly. How many times did one have to state something to convince oneself? A study of hypnotism might be in order.

"Beg pardon. My mistake." Jack smirked.

"Two days from now, seven p.m.," Lydia ordered. "Have the unwrapping instructions memorized. That's all I'm going to say on the matter." She discarded vengeful Lydia and put on proper hostess Lydia. "Now, who would like some tea?"

12
KHEPRI
scarab beetle god of rebirth

JACK NEARLY LEAPT OUT of the hack before it rattled to a stop in front of the Curiosity Club.

"Lydia," he gasped. "Is this…"

She stepped carefully down from the vehicle and waited for the driver to climb out and help unload the mummy.

"Yes. The location of our parents' club."

"Jesus." Jack shuddered. "I'm not certain I want to go inside."

"It's nothing like it was," she reassured him. "No memories. I've seen the whole building. I wouldn't have brought you if it were painful. And I thought you knew. Didn't you recognize the name Millerson?"

"No. Should I have?"

The driver dragged the mummy box from the cab and plunked it down unceremoniously. Lydia handed him a coin and he hopped back into his vehicle, leaving her and Jack standing alone before the club.

"Adolphus Millerson is the speculator who bought up the ruins of our club," she explained. "Built the new building. It's passed through several different owners since then, and had many improvements made. But now it's back in his hands."

Jack folded his arms across his chest and frowned at her. "So you want to curse the place? Why?"

Lydia sighed in exasperation. How could he not know these details? "Millerson did more than buy the club. Once, he owned several establishments. He was the man who had you thrown in prison."

Jack said nothing, but a faraway look came into his eyes. Goddammit! She hadn't wanted to remind him of that time, but how else could she explain?

"You were a boy," she spat. "He could have merely taken your money and tossed you out. Or charged you with the small crime it was. But he threw every accusation he could think of at you, half of them wholly untrue."

He had you locked in Newgate, where you nearly died, alone and terrified.

A cascade of memories crashed down on her. Tracking down Millerson. Banging on his door. Begging the guards at the prison to allow her to visit, only to be turned away and told cousins weren't close family. As if family only meant blood. As if Jack hadn't been her only love in the world.

"Shit, Lydia, you look like you've seen a ghost." He squeezed his eyes closed for a second. "Let's not dwell on this."

She breathed deeply, hating that she'd hurt both herself and him. They didn't talk about that time, and this was why. Now it was too late to stuff the memories back into the dark corners of her mind where they usually lurked.

But she would persevere. She always had. After all, it was when Jack had been in prison that she'd invented Madame Xyla. She'd told fortunes. Made predictions of wealth or love or better days ahead. Given people happiness.

She'd made them smile because she couldn't smile herself.

"You take that end," she jerked a hand toward the box sitting on the pavement.

"One moment." Jack glowered down at the mummy. "You're telling me this mummy is part of some revenge plot?"

"It's doing what should have been done years ago."

He huffed. "And what about Millerson the younger?"

"This has nothing to do with him." He would be better off without his father begging him for money and favors, in any case.

Jack rubbed his temple. "Lydia, you know I would do anything for you, but—"

"Good. Then do it. Help me carry this mummy inside."

"I don't want you to have any regrets."

Lydia stared him down until he bent to grasp one end of the coffin.

"I won't," she insisted.

~⌒

"Looks good, eh?" Adolphus Millerson gestured at the temporarily modified card room. All the tables save one had been hauled away, leaving only chairs arranged in haphazard semi-circles on each side of the room. The lone table sat in the center, beside the sphinx fountain.

Max gave a slight grunt that his father would hopefully interpret as agreement. He wouldn't have even bothered to come tonight except for Lydia. If she needed any assistance, Max wanted to be there to provide it. He'd worried more about which waistcoat to wear than about the setup of the room. Quite a bit more, in fact.

A shuffling in the hall made him turn toward the door. She was here.

Lydia, dressed in the bright, flowing garb and dark-brown wig of Madame Xyla, backed into the room, her arms clutching one end of the mummy's coffin. Max started toward her.

His father caught him by the wrist. "Let them be, son."

Max tried to shake him off. "Excuse me?"

"They are the help," his father explained, as if speaking to a child. "Do not debase yourself by partaking in their work."

"*I* am the help," Max hissed. "Need I remind you that in my professional life I'm a lowly secretary?"

"To the richest man in England. Tell him to join the club. Tell those actresses you know to have their protectors join. Once we have a few peers as members, money will roll in."

Max twisted free of his father's grasp, in no mood to cater

to his delusions. He crossed the room to assist Lydia and her cousin with the mummy, but arrived only in time to help set it down beside the table.

"Welcome," Max greeted them. "Is there anything I can help with? Anything you need?"

"It's all in the box with the mummy," Jack Weaver replied. "My cousin is extremely prepared, as always."

That brought a smile to Max's face. Yes, she was. Lydia was a woman who clearly thought things through. Her entire appearance today spoke to that. The drapy, shimmering fabrics had an ethereal quality to them, and were cut in a matronly style. She had darkened her lashes to accentuate her eyes, and traded her usual rose lip paint for a wine color. Gold—or more likely gilded—jewelry hung about her neck and dangled from her ears. She looked older. Wiser. And foreign, in a non-specific way. The costume may have appeared false on someone else, but on Lydia it was natural. She *was* Madame Xyla, spiritualist.

"Everything we need is in the box," she stated. "We will want to cover the table with the cloth, then place the mummy directly on top and store the box elsewhere. No distractions. We want as few wandering gazes as possible."

"Can you keep an eye on them, Maxwell?" his father called. "I'm feeling peckish. Think I'll go downstairs for a drink and a sandwich before we begin."

Max gave his father a nod. Best to have him somewhere else so he wouldn't say more embarrassing or insulting things.

Lydia popped the top off the mummy's coffin and pulled out a folded length of deep purple cloth. As she set about draping it over the table, Jack surveyed the area.

"People in some places will need to stand," he observed. "This… unique and interesting fountain blocks the view from a number of spots. And it makes noise. Do you think we can turn it off?"

"I can find out," Max replied.

Jack plunged a hand into the water and fished out a

handful of coins. "Perhaps we can wish it away." He tossed a farthing back. "I wish the sphinx would go elsewhere." Another farthing. "I wish it would turn invisible." Coin after coin plunked into the fountain. "Doesn't seem to be working. Do we need to answer a riddle first?"

Max chuckled. "Or perhaps those coins are devoid of wishes. Try using one of your own."

Jack gave him a look of mock horror. "I never wish with my own money. The very idea." He tossed another farthing into the water, leaving only a single coin in his hand. "I wish for great riches." He closed his fist around the small coin, and when he opened his hand again, a gold sovereign sat in the center of his palm. "There. It works."

"Nicely done," Max applauded. "Do you have any tips? I can never seem to hold my hand quite right when palming a coin. People always notice."

Jack stepped closer to demonstrate. "The key is to practice every motion with and without the coin. If I want to remove it from my pocket like this—"

Lydia cleared her throat. Max jumped.

"Right. Yes. Business," he babbled. "Let's set the mummy on the table."

He and Jack lifted the mummy from the coffin and placed it in the very center of the plum-colored tablecloth. Lydia had scattered dried leaves across the tabletop. Herbs, perhaps? Max sniffed, but didn't smell anything aromatic. It looked nice, even if she'd simply plucked it off someone's shrubbery.

Lydia opened a small vial of salt, and sprinkled it among the leaves. "We want it to appear as if we have spiritually prepared a place for this event. It will give my presence here legitimacy and create a sense of spectacle in the viewers' minds."

Jack waggled his eyebrows. "And then I will hold their attention as I perform a spectacular feat of faux archaeology."

"I don't doubt it," Max replied. Jack Weaver clearly knew

how to put on a show. Like Lydia, he would have done well on the stage.

"Don't let him seduce you with his charm," Lydia warned. "Jack is an unrepentant scoundrel. He pocketed half the coins he took from the fountain, you know."

"Would I do that?" Jack protested. Several coins splashed into the water. "Oh. Apparently, I would."

Max laughed.

Lydia rolled her eyes. The exasperated body language wasn't at all fitting for her Madame Xyla act, yet even in her costume it looked natural. A small hint of a smile tugged at her lips. Any annoyance she felt was tempered with genuine affection.

Max glanced back at Jack, struck with a new appreciation for the irreverent man. Jack's antics weren't merely for the fun of breaking rules. He was making his cousin smile. Coaxing out the fun-loving side of her Max had seen at the theater.

The theater. A shiver of desire swept across his body.

Try as he might, he couldn't stop thinking about that near kiss. What might have happened if Mrs. Pugh had waited a few more minutes to make her arrival? Max would have had Lydia in his arms. He would know the taste of her lips.

The thought that he may have missed his only opportunity made his insides twist.

Business. Focus on the business. After tonight, he could spare a thought for other things.

With the mummy situated on the table, Jack practiced addressing a crowd, while Lydia walked from place to place in the room, calling out tips on how loud to speak or which direction to face. By the time they finished, the very first of the attendees began to trickle in. Max's father returned, drink in hand, and lounged against the wall, looking smug.

At two minutes after eight p.m., Lydia began the performance.

"Good evening, gentlemen, and welcome to this unique

experience of the spiritual and the scientific. I am Madame Xyla." She paused. Her name was well enough known that many would recognize it. "The Curiosity Club has prepared your surroundings for an evening sure to amaze. The cards call for a night of surprises. Astonishment awaits us all. Enjoy the event and allow me to introduce our expert archaeologist, Mr. Jack Worthington-Price."

Lydia sat, and Jack nodded to the crowd with the cool sophistication one might expect of a scholar named Worthington-Price. He brandished a gleaming knife.

"Let us begin, gentlemen. With these old and fragile bindings, it is unrealistic to think we might pick up our mummified friend, twirl him around, and unwrap him in one long strip."

The audience chuckled.

"I will therefore be making careful incisions at strategic locations, peeling back the wrappings, and revealing what is beneath bit-by-bit. We shall begin here." Jack touched the tip of the knife to the mummy.

Max couldn't tell whether Jack had truly read scholarly papers about Ancient Egyptian burial practices or not. The words slipping from his lips sounded confident and erudite, which was all that mattered. Good to his word, he held the attention of the attendees.

Max, though, watched Lydia. In an ideal world, he would have been close enough to lean toward her and whisper. He would have liked to exchange commentary on Jack's performance. But she was here in her professional capacity, and as far as anyone else knew, Max was part of the audience.

She sat still, but not rigidly, becoming part of the backdrop, even in her eye-catching costume. Patient and circumspect. A performer who knew when and how to share the stage. Many did not.

Max's gaze lingered on her face. Her ability to retain an

impassive facade truly was remarkable. It was no wonder she could wager at cards with such skill.

Without warning, her composure snapped. Her eyes widened and her lips parted. Jack let out a yelp of surprise.

Max's eyes darted to the mummy. In the center of the torso, where Jack had begun peeling away the wrappings, crawled a shiny black beetle, nearly an inch long.

Jack recovered quickly, flicking the insect away with the tip of the knife. It landed in a man's lap, causing him to cry out and leap to his feet, swiping the small creature to the floor.

"These decaying artifacts attract visitors now and then," Jack announced calmly. "No harm done."

The audience chuckled. Max glanced at his father. Adolphus Millerson had straightened up and his smug smile was now tight.

Jack continued as if nothing untoward had happened. He sliced further into the mummy and peeled back a larger section of the bandages. "Now, here we will find—"

Lydia gasped. Jack leapt backward and nearly dropped the knife as a swarm of beetles burst from the mummy's chest. Several men sitting close by cried out in alarm. One man tipped his chair over, knocking down two others as he fell. People began to shout. The insects scattered. Hollow thumps echoed from somewhere in the distance. Someone, somewhere, moaned.

"A curse!" a voice shrieked. "It's the sacred beetles!"

Others joined in.

"Scarabs! Thousands of them!"

"They feast on human flesh!"

"They're protecting the mummy! It's cursed! The mummy is cursed!"

The room erupted into panic. Beetles poured over the edge of the table and tumbled to the floor. Men ran for the door, pushing and shoving, flinging one another aside. A few shouted for calm. Some stood staring at the floor in horror, stomping uselessly at dots of color on the patterned carpet.

"Don't be alarmed," Max's father called out, his voice unusually high-pitched. He was too late. Anything else he said was lost in the general hubbub.

Max hopped from his seat and rushed to the table. He caught one of the insects between his thumb and forefinger and lifted it up for inspection.

"It's only a common beetle." He could do nothing to save the event, now that the entire audience was fleeing for the exit. But he could analyze the situation rationally. "Not an ancient scarab." And there were hardly thousands of them. Not even hundreds. Perhaps a few dozen, and already they had mostly disappeared in the chaos.

Lydia's nose wrinkled in distaste as she peered at the bug, but she didn't flinch away. "Interesting booby trap."

Max turned back to the crowd. The majority had already made it out the door. The rest were filing out in an orderly fashion, heads shaking. Max's father made pleading protests, but few men heeded him.

Max looked back down at the beetle wriggling in his grasp. He tossed it onto the floor, and it skittered away into the nearest dark corner. He moved closer to Lydia and said in a low voice, "Perhaps we need to have a talk with your mummy supplier."

"I don't recommend having a talk with Julian Carter," Jack cut in. "The man thrives on chaos. I wouldn't be surprised if he was here, watching. Probably the one making those moaning noises." He shrugged and bent to slide the mummy's coffin out from beneath the table. "May as well clean up, I suppose. The event may have been cut short, but no one can say we didn't give them a hell of a show."

Only a few men remained behind in the room now. A pair of stragglers stood in a corner, talking with Max's father.

Adolphus Millerson, face crimson, swiped a furious gesture at the mummy.

Max's stomach lurched. He grabbed Jack's arm to halt him.

"Leave it. I'll clean everything." He turned to look Lydia in the eye. "You should go, before my father blames this mess on you."

An odd expression passed over her face. One he'd never seen before. Her lips were pinched, her lids partially lowered. Did she feel guilty about this?

She quickly schooled her features. "Come with us," she said. "This was *his* terrible idea. Let him deal with the aftermath. You shouldn't have to clean up after his mess."

The truth stung. Max didn't want to be here. He didn't want to be doing this. But he'd been cleaning up after his father's messes since he was seventeen years old, so he shook his head.

"It's fine. I can manage."

Their gazes locked for a long moment. The instant he thought she would turn away, she darted in and planted a firm kiss directly on his lips. Then she whirled around, yanked her purple tablecloth from beneath the mummy, and walked quickly, but regally, toward the exit. Jack hurried after.

Max stared until she vanished from sight. His lips tingled. A touch of cinnamon scent lingered in the air around him. Fiery tongues of longing coursed through his body. The kiss had lasted but a second, but in that second, she'd upended his entire world.

"Damnation," he breathed.

Why the devil hadn't he gone with her?

13
KHONSU
god of the moon

A loud rap on the door startled Max out of his daydream. The paper he was holding—sadly, a contract with an insurance company rather than a salacious letter—slipped from his grasp and fluttered to the floor.

"Come in." Max called. Heaving a sigh, he bent to retrieve the paper. He ought to be concentrating on work, he supposed. At least this time he'd been interrupted before he veered off into more fantasies of kissing spiritualists.

A young maid in a black dress and dusty apron stepped into the room and curtsied. "Excuse me, sir. There's a delivery outside, and I'm sent to tell you there's some trouble with it and you're needed. Sorry to interrupt you, sir."

Max gave her a reassuring smile. "It's no trouble. I'll be right out."

The girl bobbed another curtsy and scampered off. Max had been working here for years and still couldn't accustom himself to the deferential treatment the cleaning staff offered him. Secretary occupied a strange in-between position, not quite a gentleman, not quite a servant. Max disliked the bowing and scraping when he was the recipient as much as he disliked doing it.

That, coupled with the perpetual boredom, was why he loathed this job.

You should quit.

"I can't quit," he said aloud, ignoring the nagging sensation that never quite seemed to disappear. This job kept him fed, it wasn't arduous, and when he went home at the end of the day, he retained the physical and mental capacity to work on his plays. His family relied on his continued employment.

Max walked through the corridor, past Mr. Black's office, which, as usual, remained resolutely closed, and out to the front door. An irate delivery man stood beside a crate that measured three feet in every direction. Mr. Black certainly hadn't ordered anything so large. Max would have handled the paperwork himself.

"Now, see here," the delivery man growled. He waved a piece of paper. "This crate needs to be signed for, or I don't get paid. I've got a whole wagon of goods to deliver, and I won't be waiting around all day!"

Max summoned up his best professional calm. Compared to procuring a mummy, this was the simplest of problems. He'd fix it. He always fixed things. Even if it was slowly sucking the life out of him.

Minutes later, they had the issue resolved: the address on the paper didn't match the one hastily scrawled on the side of the crate. The delivery belonged a few doors down. Max was helping the delivery man hoist the crate back onto his wagon, when a familiar, confident stride caught his eye. He faltered and clumsily set down his side of the box.

"Back to your desk work, lad," the delivery man chuckled.

"Uh-huh," Max replied, his gaze locked on Lydia.

She came to an abrupt halt when she spied him, then lifted a hand in greeting. Max strode toward her.

"Ly— Miss Weaver," he corrected himself. "Good afternoon."

Lydia resumed her stride, swiftly closing the distance between them. "Good afternoon. I didn't expect to see you here."

"I work here." Max waved a hand at the tall building behind him. "Uh, as you know."

"Yes." She didn't fidget, but her cheeks were flushed pink. Maybe he wasn't the only one flustered by this unexpected meeting. "I was out for a walk. And the post office isn't far from here."

"Yes, of course." A walk. The flush on her face was only from the exercise. Not bashfulness, and certainly not desire. Max stuffed his hands in his pockets. "How are you?"

"Well. You?"

"Also well." Good Lord. This was the most inane conversation. All he needed to do was mention the weather and he would confirm his place as the dullest man in London.

"I'm glad to hear that. Your father didn't blame you for the curse, did he?"

Max shook his head emphatically. "No. Nothing like that. He said very little about it, in fact." Max wasn't sure whether his father was embarrassed about the event or merely baffled by what had transpired. Either way, Max hoped he would think twice before hosting another such event.

"Good." Lydia's expression hardened. "You don't deserve to take the blame for his foolishness."

An awkward silence fell. Max groped for a topic that had nothing to do with the club, his job, or the weather. The only thing that came to mind was how lovely Lydia looked today, in sky blue trimmed with white. She reminded him of a beautiful, sunny day.

"I heard a new show is premiering at your theater," she broke the silence. "Has *Scarlet and the Wolf* finished its run?"

Perfect. This, Max could talk about. "No. The owner likes to have the theater run two shows on alternating days when possible. He thinks it brings in a wider audience. Rarely do we have scenery so elaborate it can't be swapped in and out. In this case, the new play is sharing most of the same sets. It's a comedic farce, I believe."

"You haven't seen it yet?" Lydia asked.

"No."

"The comment I saw in the paper said it's quite funny. Would you like to join me for tomorrow's performance? We can discover if it lives up to the talk."

"I'd love to," Max blurted. A play *and* Lydia's company? Who could turn down such an offer? He hadn't expected to have a chance to spend time with her in a situation entirely removed from their business arrangement. He wasn't going to waste this one. Especially when it presented the possibility for another, longer kiss. "Shall I pick you up at your house? Seven p.m.?"

"That sounds perfect. I will let you return to your work. Have a good day, Mr. Millerson."

He inclined his head. "Until tomorrow."

What had she been thinking?

Lydia considered, then discarded, yet another pair of earrings. Too big. She didn't want anything that drew attention away from her dress. The midnight blue silk with silver accents was the most beautiful dress she'd ever owned. The long, snug bodice accentuated the hour-glass shape of her body. The skirt was a cascading ripple of elegant folds. She was a pond at midnight, sparkling in the moonlight.

She tried another pair of earrings. Simple pearls. They would do. Now all that remained was the problem of her hair.

Dammit, Lydia.

She was fussing overmuch. She knew it, knew it was unnecessary and silly, yet she couldn't seem to stop. Her head hadn't been in the right place since she'd kissed Max Millerson.

Why? Why had she done that?

Lydia frowned at her reflection. She knew why. She was wildly attracted to him, and in that moment it had seemed like her only chance for a taste.

It's more than that and you know it, she chided herself. *You want him to want you. To think well of you. And not to blame you for the curse on the club.*

Her gaze drifted to the newspaper clipping resting nearby. "Mummy Curses Curiosity Club," the headline read. People were talking, and the result was everything she'd hoped. She skimmed down to the last line of the article. "Whether a real curse or a practical joke, one thing is certain: Lady Luck was not smiling on the Curiosity Club."

It was perfect. Gamblers hated anything that carried even a suggestion of bad luck. Some men would stay away. Others would begin to blame every poor hand at cards on the mummy's curse. Soon Adolphus Millerson would have no choice but to beg for spiritual intervention. And when he did, Madame Xyla would be there.

The doorbell rang. Blast! She still hadn't finished with her hair.

"I'll answer it!" Jack shouted from downstairs. Racing footsteps pounded across the floor. The front door creaked open. "Evening, Millerson," Jack said, loudly enough that Lydia could hear his words clearly. "Step inside. Lydia is upstairs primping. I think she's taking extra time to be certain to look her best."

Lydia rose from her dressing table, stalked across the room, and closed her door. She was in no mood for Jack's teasing. She returned to the mirror and picked up her hairbrush.

Her unruly blond curls hung just to her ears. Too short to pin. She always looked tousled, even after a good brushing. Lydia flicked a stray lock back from her forehead. Nothing more to be done about it, she supposed.

She checked over her dress one final time, making certain no threads were hanging off and she hadn't missed any buttons. All in order. No more excuses. She picked up the small silver purse where she'd stashed her house key and a few coins, and tied it securely at her hip. Time to go.

Lydia slipped from her room and started down the stairs. Half-way down, she paused. Jack and Max still waited for her in the front hall, but their conversation had moved on from her tardiness. Both men had taken a knee in the center of the space. Jack's black cat, Phantom, who usually kept out of sight, stood between them, arching into Max's hand as he petted her sleek fur.

"You're a sweet kitty," he cooed.

"She's fond of sandwiches." Jack produced a sandwich from his pocket and presented it to the cat, who pawed at it before taking a bite. "Turkey is a favorite. And if you want her to play, shiny, dangly things are best. I have a spare pocket watch for a cat toy."

Phantom ate another bite of the sandwich, then decided she'd had enough attention and raced off toward the kitchen.

"She fits right in with the family," Max declared. "A definite mind of her own and utterly charming."

Jack put a hand to his heart. "You flatter me."

Max laughed.

Lydia cleared her throat. The men looked up. Max jumped

to his feet. His bronze-colored eyes sparkled, and a wide smile dimpled his cheeks.

"Miss Weaver. What a lovely dress. Are you ready for our outing?"

"Yes, I am, thank you."

"Capital. Let's be on our way." He picked up his hat from the small table by the door and set it on his head. When Lydia joined him, he offered his arm, but when her fingers pressed against his biceps, he winced.

Lydia sprang back. "Did I hurt you?" Yes, she was tense this evening, but she hadn't thought she'd grasped him particularly hard. Usually she had better control than that.

"Oh, it's only a bruise," Max reassured her. "From when you whacked me with that sword."

"That was almost a week ago," she exclaimed.

"Well, it was quite a solid blow. It's only tender to the touch now. And it's turned a remarkable combination of green and yellow. Would you like to see it?"

Behind them, Jack snickered.

"My apologies," Max hurriedly added. "That was inappropriate. I'm overly accustomed to the theater, where everyone is continually dressing and undressing."

"No apology needed." Lydia took his arm again, more carefully this time, and ushered him out the door. He certainly didn't need to hold his tongue on her behalf. Although she wasn't sure she wanted him conjuring up fantasies where he removed his clothing, either.

Wrong. She did want that. But in that direction lay all sorts of complications.

"Have fun, Lydia," Jack called after her. "Don't stay out too late. Or if you do, I want to hear all the salacious details in the morning!"

Lydia never told anyone such things. Ever. Not that it mattered. Nothing salacious would be happening. This was a friendly outing only. Never mind the tingle in her body from a mere touch.

This was a terrible idea. What had she been thinking?

The theater was abuzz with activity tonight. Ladies and gents from all walks of life swarmed the building in their colorful evening attire, eager to take in a show, escape from ordinary life, and enjoy a good laugh.

The seats Lydia and Max had procured were by no means the best, but neither were they shabby. The theater's design allowed for a good view from most locations, and Lydia already knew about the excellent stage lighting. She settled in and prepared for an evening of fun.

As it happened, most of the fun came from whispering to Max. While many people around them laughed uproariously, for Lydia most of the jokes fell flat. The play wasn't bad, but it wasn't at all her style of humor. She liked wordplay, irony, and character humor, such as in *Scarlet and the Wolf.* This play was entirely contrived situations and slapstick, which she preferred in small doses.

She leaned toward Max, bumping his shoulder with hers. Again. She couldn't seem to stop the fleeting, semi-accidental touches. Her body craved each tiny sensation.

"I want there to be a magical explanation for the number of comical falls," she whispered.

His head turned toward her, and the heat of his breath made the tiny hairs on her neck stand on end. "Agreed. Have the characters been cursed with clumsiness, or has the ground been turned to ice?"

As a man and a woman onstage collided, the mask the woman was wearing flew off. The two characters gaped at one another.

"It's you!" the man exclaimed.

The stage lights went dark and the audience burst into applause.

When the house lights brightened, Max and Lydia rose

from their seats and headed out to the main hall, meandering through the throng of chattering people.

"Do you want to stay for the second half?" he asked.

Lydia mulled over the question a moment. "Maybe. I'm enjoying myself, but it's not my sort of show. Your commentary was more amusing to me."

A slight blush stole over his cheeks. Oh, dear. It was entirely unfair for a man to be so lovely. He did terrible, unsettling things to Lydia's too-long celibate body.

"You're too kind," he replied. "Would you like to visit backstage, instead? Watch some of the action behind the scenes?"

Lydia grinned, remembering the lights and the props and the sword fighting. "I'd love that, thank you."

Max led her through the theater to a door guarded by a short, but well-muscled man.

"Hallo, M.," he said, giving a gap-toothed smile. "Bringing your lady for a tour?" He opened the door. "You know the rules. Keep out of everyone's way and off the stage."

Max and Lydia passed through the door and into the back hall he'd shown her the other day. Tonight it was jammed with actors, many of them half-dressed. They talked and fussed, checking costumes and makeup, preparing for the second half of the show. Max led Lydia to a clear spot against the wall, where they could wait and watch the activity.

"We'll stay here until the play starts up again, and then we can walk around," he suggested.

Lydia nodded, content to observe. The busy, boisterous atmosphere reminded her in some ways of the gaming club of her youth. People moving here and there, the mixture of hard work and entertainment, the freedom from strict social rules.

As she eyed the men and women at work, a familiar figure caught her eye. Tall and blond, with piercing dark eyes, his handsome features stood out even among many attractive faces. He was older now, a man in his prime, but still very much as she remembered. His gaze swept past her without recognition, only to snap back suddenly.

"Lydia?"

"Thomas Pondthistle," she greeted him. "It's been a long time."

He hurried over, putting a finger to his lips in a shushing motion. "Don't use that name," he hissed. "It's Glastonbury now. Irving Glastonbury."

"Pondthistle?" Max smothered a snort. "No wonder you don't use that name."

"Hush," Tom—Irving said. "A man needs something debonair if he's to be on the stage."

"So you're an actor now," Lydia mused. It made sense. She hadn't known him long, but he'd been a large presence and a natural charmer. "Good for you."

"Thank you." Irving tipped the wide-brimmed hat he wore with his costume. He was playing an American cowboy, it appeared. "And you. You're..." He looked from Lydia to Max and then back again. "Blimey! Are you Max's spiritualist? *You're* Madame Xyla?"

"I am."

"Huh." Irving reached a hand beneath his hat and scratched his head.

Max gave him a confused look. "Irv, you know Miss Weaver? And somehow didn't know she was Madame Xyla?"

"Well..." Irv shrugged. "She looks different with the wig and the jewels and all. I only saw Madame Xyla at one performance, and it was from across a room."

Max's brow furrowed even further. "She looks the same to me no matter what she's wearing. I can pick her out from fifty yards away by the way she walks. I don't understand."

Irv clapped him on the shoulder. "You obviously already know her better than I ever did. Show's about to start. I should go. You two enjoy one another." The suggestive waggle of his eyebrows left no doubt as to his meaning. He tipped his hat again and departed through the stage door.

Lydia turned to Max. "You know me from the way I walk?"

"From all your movements, in fact," Max explained. "You have a very distinctive bearing. Full of confidence and energy. It's elegant, but also has something fierce—"

"Stop." She raised a hand to cut him off. If he continued on in this manner she was going to kiss him again, and she wasn't certain if she wanted that.

Her gaze flicked toward the stage. Actually… She'd been infatuated with Irv, once upon a time. They'd had a fling, she'd had a great time, and then she'd been done. Satisfied. No longer hanging on his every word and thrilling to his every touch.

Maybe a kiss was exactly what she needed now. She could have a bit of fun, take Max to her bed, and when it was over with, she would cease thinking of him night and day. She would never again have to worry that she would find herself wandering unconsciously toward his place or work or that she might impulsively ask him to the theater. She would move on and return to her plans with nothing more to distract her.

The lights dimmed and the hall grew quiet. Only a few steps away was a dark, deserted dressing room. Lydia took hold of Max's lapels and dragged him inside.

14
KEK

god of darkness

The door banged closed. Max went willingly as Lydia steered him deeper into the dark chamber and backed him up against a wall. "Did I say something wrong?" he asked. "Or—"

Her hands lifted to thread through his hair.

"Or right?"

He bent toward her and she rose to meet him, bringing their mouths together in a scorching kiss. Bloody hell. This was the kiss in the club multiplied a thousand times. A kiss to alter fate. A kiss to launch a thousand ships. Somewhere, choirs of angels were singing about this kiss.

What was it he'd said about her movements? Elegant, but fierce? Exactly that. Lydia's lips were soft against his, warm, and inviting. There was a possession, though, in the way her mouth covered his, and the way her tongue swept inside him. She was claiming him, branding him. Not with force, but with passion.

Lord, the passion. He'd seen the spark in her eyes and the coiled energy beneath her firm control. To feel it, though, was to have one's world shaken. Her body undulated against his, never still, her fingers sliding over his scalp, her tongue darting and teasing and tempting.

Max flattened his hands against her back and drew her snugly against him, reveling in the sway of her hips and the brush of her breasts across his chest. When he tipped his head slightly for a different angle, she ceded some of her control to him without hesitation. Max delved deeper, stroking her tongue, tasting her essence, while his hands began to rove up and down her back. Lydia allowed him access, her body arching to accommodate his actions. Slight gasps of pleasure encouraged him to go further.

Fuck, but she was delicious. Confident in her sexuality. Comfortable with her power. Not afraid to take what she wanted or accept what he offered.

"Lydia," he groaned. He dragged his mouth away from hers, bending further to nuzzle her neck and taste the soft skin just above her collar.

She tugged him away from the wall, giving her room to stroke down his back and squeeze his buttocks. Max dropped his hands lower and returned the favor.

Dammit, he wanted her, right here, right now. He wanted to fling up her skirts and bury himself inside her. He wanted to strip her bare and kiss every part of her body.

"You're fucking gorgeous," he rasped, kneading her backside and grinding his hips into hers.

"You can hardly see me," she teased, tilting her head to expose more of her neck to him.

"Doesn't matter. I remember you." God, her arse was luscious beneath his fingers. Round and plump and perfect. Maybe he ought to find one of the dressing tables and bend her over it so he could see it bare while he drove into her.

"I remember every curve," he continued. "Hugged by midnight silk. Sparkling like the night sky."

A whimper of pleasure came from her throat and she rocked her pelvis into his. "I wore it for you," she panted. "Knew you'd like it."

"I love it." He released her and brought his hands to her torso, where a row of tiny buttons ran down the front of her bodice. His fingers groped for the top button, poking it carefully through the hole. "I want to peel it from your body, inch-by-inch."

Lydia reached for his necktie, her nimble fingers unknotting it in seconds. "Only if I can do the same to you."

"Please."

Slowly, they began to undress one another, trading button for button, one portion of exposed skin for another. In the unlit room, they sank into the sense of touch, dragging their fingers over each newfound patch of flesh.

Electric sizzles radiated out from every place Lydia's fingers grazed him. His breathing had gone ragged. Hell, if he didn't have her soon he might combust.

He slid a hand inside her half-open bodice, down beneath the layers to her corset. Stiff boning. Soft breasts beneath. Her wriggle and gasp when he stroked her told him that she, too, was adrift in this swirl of contrasting sensations.

Yes. Let go. Lose yourself with me.

Lydia splayed her own hand against Max's chest, finding his nipple and teasing it with one finger. He dropped a hand to her skirts, tugging upward. The damned slim style hampered him. He worked his other hand free from her bodice to help. He needed more of her. All of her.

Max tried to turn them around without letting go. Maybe if he found a wall they could brace against...

His elbow smacked into something hard, sending a sharp spear of pain down his arm. He yelped and stumbled, crashing into whatever he had bumped.

A dressing screen. He could tell by the way it rattled and folded in on itself as it collapsed beneath him. He slipped from Lydia's grasp and tumbled to the floor in a tangle of flailing limbs and snapping wood.

"Well, shite," he grumbled. He'd have to pay for that.

As he tried to collect himself, Lydia moved away from him. He heard her fumbling, and then a match flared. She lit the gas lamp by the door and turned it up to illuminate the room.

"Max? Are you hurt?"

"No." He struggled to his feet, rubbing his sore elbow. The tingling in his arm had mostly abated. "I appear to have murdered a privacy screen, though."

"That can be replaced. You can't."

"I'm fine," he assured her.

"Good." She adjusted her bodice and began to refasten her buttons. "Something about this theater seems to promote taking leave of one's senses. Perhaps the casual debauchery thespians are known for has left the building with a metaphysical residue of unchecked hedonism."

Max bent to retrieve his necktie from the floor, hiding his disappointed frown from her view. He'd been quite enjoying the unchecked hedonism. But she had a reputation to maintain, he supposed. Spiritualist was a respectable position. Cavorting at the theater was probably not wise.

"I don't believe in metaphysical whatchamacallit," he replied. "Although a spiritualist did once tell me I would find the partner I needed and she was right." His own words brought a smile back to his face and he looked at Lydia again. Maybe they oughtn't be lovers, despite how much he wanted her. But they could be friends, couldn't they?

Her blond eyebrows arched and her lips twitched in an unmistakably seductive smile. "Perhaps The Lovers was meant to be interpreted more literally than I had anticipated," she purred. She closed the space between them and trailed a finger down his chest where his shirt still gaped open. "This is not the place, but we should see each other again. In private. We should make arrangements."

Max sucked in a sharp breath, then let it out slowly. "Tell me when and where. I'll be there."

15
QETESH
goddess of sacred ecstasy and sexual pleasure

Brown was not Lydia's color. But at least she was getting more use out of this dress than the one visit to the Curiosity Club. Lord knew, she wasn't going to wear it on any normal day. Besides, she wouldn't have to wear it much longer.

Max's flat was in a not-quite-middle-class area a few streets away from the theater. The buildings were tidy, but by no means fancy. No one here would take much notice of a woman rapping on a man's door late at night. The rough, low-cut dress made her fit in all the more.

Lydia tugged on the hood of her capelet, making certain her short blond hair remained concealed. She had no intention of deviating from her course of action, but discretion was vital. If her reputation became tainted, her position as Madame Xyla would be in jeopardy. Fortunately, though it had been some years since she'd visited a man in this fashion, she had not forgotten how to avoid notice. This plan was far better and safer than jumping him in a theater dressing room.

Max lived in the upstairs flat of the small building. Lydia found the main entrance unlocked, so she entered and walked up the stairs to rap directly on his door. He answered promptly. Lydia slipped inside, only lowering her hood once the door had been closed behind her. The room was a simple, all-purpose space, with a table and chairs for dining, a couch, and several bookshelves. An open door led to a second room, where Lydia could glimpse a small corner of the bed.

"Welcome." Max took her cape and hung it on a peg.

His gaze traveled up and down her body. "In disguise again tonight?"

Lydia nodded. "It was necessary. It's frustratingly less convenient when your lover is a man." Her last two lovers had been women. Everyone assumed visits were only between friends. How naive. Or perhaps willfully ignorant.

Max considered her words a moment. He was neither naive nor ignorant. Nor surprised, it seemed. "Yes. I can see how it would be. Thank you for visiting, despite the bother."

She gave him a sly smile. "I believe it will be well worth the bother, for both of us."

"I hope so." He glanced around the room, then stuffed his hands in his pockets. Nervous.

Why did she find that strangely attractive? It didn't matter, she supposed. Soon she would fulfill all her lustful fantasies of him, and then she would no longer be drawn to every little thing he did.

"I… probably should have prepared something," he said, nodding at her unattractive dress. "You clearly planned. I ought to have, what? Answered the door naked? Or had brandy to offer you. Flowers? My apologies. I'm clearly better suited to spontaneity. You'd think this was my first time."

Lydia chuckled. "I know it's not your first time. You *are* friends with Irving Glastonbury. No one can do that for long and remain inexperienced."

"Oh, have you slept with him too? He does seductive charm rather well."

"Yes, but I was actually thinking of the way he tries to ensure his friends never lack for companionship."

Max turned a bright shade of red. "Ah. Yes. And once again I've said something inappropriate."

Lydia couldn't deny he did that often. His tongue was very free around her, and not only while they were kissing. She had to conclude that he felt a similar level of comfort with her as he did with his friends.

Does that mean we're friends? She shook the thought off.

"Discussing sexual dalliances is hardly inappropriate," she said. "Considering what we're about to do."

His face relaxed into a smile. "An excellent point. May as well lay all cards on the table. No innocents here. We've both shagged the same chap. I'm terrible at planned seduction. And I'd best make this good for you, because you had to sneak here and risk being caught out. I believe that covers everything. Also, your tits are quite fabulous, even if your dress is not."

Lydia's entire body warmed. Max would never be a suave seducer, but he was utterly charming in his own way. Blunt. Honest. Open-minded. He'd shown absolutely no signs of jealousy at the mention of her previous lovers. Nothing. Not even a twitch. It was refreshing. Enticing. Oddly arousing.

For pity's sake, Lydia, stop mooning over him and get on with it. You need to get this infatuation out of your system.

She gestured toward the bedroom. "Would you like a closer look?"

"Obviously."

Max's bedroom was small and cluttered. Most of one wall was taken up by a large wardrobe. Its doors were open, revealing an array of shirts, coats, and trousers, packed tightly together and hanging in no apparent order. Grooming supplies covered every inch of the corner washstand. The bedside table held a lamp, a notebook, a scattering of assorted papers, and three pencils. The bed itself, comfortably large enough for two, filled most of the rest of the room.

Lydia wasted no time unfastening the buttons of her dress. The garment slithered to the floor, followed quickly by her petticoat.

Max shrugged out of his coat and tossed it on the floor in front of the wardrobe. "Is this a race? I think I'm winning."

It was a silly statement. Even sillier, it roused her competitive spirit. She hastily discarded her corset cover, then popped the corset clasps open. The undergarment fell atop the growing pile of clothing. Her chemise and drawers could be off in seconds. Only her boots and stockings would take any time. She sat down on the bed and tugged at her laces.

"Care to amend that statement?" she challenged.

Max dropped his waistcoat, then began to leisurely unfasten his cuffs. "No."

Lydia's first boot hit the floor. Then the second. When she began to roll one stocking down her leg, Max stopped undressing altogether.

"I am most assuredly winning," he declared.

Lydia wadded up the stocking into a ball and threw it at him. "Take your clothes off."

He—finally—tugged his shirt free of his trousers and pulled it over his head. He smirked at her as he cast it aside. "Isn't patience a virtue?"

Lydia threw her second stocking at him. "So is chastity."

Max slipped the top button of his trousers open. "And that's no fun at all. You're right. I ought to be in a much greater hurry. The problem is, I am a devotee of the theatrical arts. I enjoy watching."

A pulse of desire throbbed between Lydia's legs. She'd give him something to watch. She shucked her chemise and drawers and sprawled naked on his bed, giving him a good look at her. She met his gaze, then cupped her breasts, kneading them and teasing her nipples to stiff peaks. Her own touch brought forth a sigh of pleasure.

Max groaned. "Christ, Lydia, you're a siren. You're going to lure me to my doom." He kicked away the last of his clothing and stood at the foot of the bed, gazing down at her, his eyes agleam in the dim lamplight. "I want to kiss you everywhere. I want to run my hands over every inch of your body. I want to pound into you until we both come apart. I want to take you every which way and back again." He tilted closer, eyes ablaze with desire, pinning her to the bed with the force of his gaze. "But what do *you* want?"

Oh, God. Her body had been hot before. Now she was melting, turning into a searing, molten puddle of need. What did she want? For him to never stop looking at her the way he was looking now.

Without warning, he stepped to the side of the bed and turned down the lamp. Then he pulled open the curtain of the room's single window. A shaft of light from the streetlamp directly outside fell across the bed.

"There," Max declared. "Now I can see you in the moonlight."

"It's a gas lamp," Lydia replied. Damn, but he had muddled her senses, for her to be stating such an obvious fact.

Max moved once again to the foot of the bed, leaning over her. "It's the moonlight. And you, my nymph, are lying on a bed of soft moss in the enchanted forest. The air is humming with magic. A cool breeze touches your skin and draws delighted shivers from your body."

"Max," she gasped. She dropped a hand between her legs, stroking her fingers through the moisture there and rubbing it across her clitoris in slow circles. "Keep talking."

His voice, already husky, dropped lower. "You sense there is someone watching you, a presence in the darkness. You cannot see him, but your ears catch words on the breeze."

"Yes." Lydia slid one finger inside herself, her legs falling open wider to give him a better view.

"'Beauty,' he whispers." His voice rasped across her skin like an erotic caress. "'Goddess. Perfection.'"

She pinched one nipple, her other hand stroking faster, pumping harder. "More."

"You turn your face to the moonlight, feeling its magic kiss on your skin. You glow beneath it, the very essence of sensuality. Soft footsteps sound on the grass as your mystery lover approaches. He is captivated—no, bewitched. Bewitched is better. He falls to his knees beside you, begging you for the honor of watching but a moment more."

Lydia's head was spinning. Max was the spellcaster here,

not her. She had fallen into the role he'd given her and now she *was* his nymph. The streetlight was her perfect moonlight, and she was lost in the fantasy they were spinning.

He climbed up to kneel on the bed beside her. "Let me watch you fly, my faerie queen."

The climax crashed over her, long and glorious, and so much better than any she'd given herself in a long, long time.

"Max," she gasped. "Oh, Max."

He bent and pressed a kiss to her forehead. "You are ethereal. Best performance I've watched in ages."

Her chest still rose and fell in heavy breaths, but she recovered enough to smile at him and let her gaze rake down his body to where his cock jutted from a thatch of dark hair.

"Yes. I see you've given me a standing ovation."

He could have groaned at that, or rolled his eyes, but his laugh was genuine. "Let me write that down." He dove for the bedside table and scribbled something on one of the many sheets of paper, then turned back to her. "Now. Act two?"

Lydia pushed up on one elbow and pointed at the place beside her. "Lie down."

He obeyed. Lydia straddled him, placing both hands on his chest and flicking her fingers over his small nipples.

"The nymph pins her admirer to the ground," she said. "Lured in by her trap, he is helpless beneath her. He has no recourse but to pleasure her for as long as she desires."

Lydia adjusted her position, sinking slowly down on Max's cock until he was fully seated inside her. His eyes slid closed and his lips parted on a gasp of ecstasy.

"He is… at her command," he panted.

"Good." Lydia began to rock, delighting in the slow, steady friction of their joined bodies. She bent over to trail kisses up Max's neck. She sucked on his earlobe until he shivered, then whispered, "Because she desires a lengthy ride."

She kissed him on the mouth, then, thrusting her tongue

between his lips in a rhythm that matched the movement of their bodies.

You are mine, mystery admirer. I have claimed you and you can never escape.

They would be trapped for eternity, here in the enchanted forest. Bliss.

Her body, though, had other ideas than "forever." A new tension had begun to build and she quickened her pace, shifting her body to position him in the perfect spot. She broke the kiss and straightened up, bracing herself with both hands as her head lolled back and her lips opened on a sigh.

This, this, this.

God, it was good. All of it, glorious. His fingers dug into her skin where he grasped her hips. He made hungry, primal sounds to match her own. Now and then he moaned her name. A plea for release.

It couldn't end. Lydia didn't want it to end. But she was close, so close, and she wanted that too. Needed it. Forever would break her.

"Lydia," Max choked out. "I— I can't—"

He didn't need to, because suddenly she was soaring, trembling, tumbling, her whole body convulsing in another earth-shattering orgasm. Max lifted her off of him, his beautiful face contorting in agonized pleasure as he finished into his hand. Lydia flopped onto her back, her heart hammering.

"Fucking hell," she murmured.

"Yes."

She tilted her head to look at Max. His chest rose and fell in deep breaths. If she pressed an ear to his chest, would his heartbeat match hers? She suspected it would.

He turned to brush a kiss over her lips. The softest, gentlest kiss she'd ever felt. So brief. But so tender. Her stomach gave an odd lurch.

"I knew we'd be magic together," Max whispered. He slid from the bed and strode to the washbasin to clean up. After wiping himself, he dampened a second cloth, then brought it to the bed and offered it to Lydia.

A considerate lover, not only during, but after. She smiled up at him from beneath lashes heavy with sleepy satisfaction.

When she'd finished, he tossed the cloth onto the pile of dirty clothes and climbed back in the bed. He reached to wrap an arm around her, pulling gently to draw her into an embrace.

Lydia didn't cuddle after sex. It wasn't something she'd ever asked for, and her previous partners hadn't offered. Coupling was a straightforward, sensible, mutually satisfying transaction. It wasn't… romantic.

And yet she made no attempt to halt Max's efforts. She allowed him to bring their bodies flush together and press kisses into her hair. When the urge to snuggle closer overtook her, she gave in. His skin was so warm and soft, his chest covered with fine hairs that tickled her breasts. With every inhalation, she caught a faint scent of tobacco and shaving soap. His fingers trailed up and down her back, not sensually, but reverently. She could fall asleep this way, safe in his arms.

"I hope I was worth the bother," he murmured, his voice heavy with drowsiness. "Maybe I can sneak… disguise… next time."

A moment later, his hands stilled. His breathing slowed. Lydia lay frozen. If she moved, would she wake him? *Should* she wake him? The siren song of Morpheus called to her.

Close your eyes. Join him.

No. No, she couldn't.

She eased herself gingerly from his grasp and climbed from the bed. She couldn't stay here. Not when he was already talking about "next time." There wasn't supposed to *be* a next time. She was supposed to go home content with everything. If she ever saw him again, she'd simply smile and say, "That was a great time we had. I'll be getting back to my revenge now, thank you."

But something was wrong. Something was definitely

wrong, because she wasn't leaving. She was gazing down on him and her heart was melting because he looked so peaceful and beautiful lying there. Lydia wanted to dive right back into the bed and hold him. She forced herself to turn away. She didn't hold people. Not outside her family.

Her gaze caught on the stack of papers at Max's bedside. Curious, she stepped closer. "Standing ovation = great innuendo," he'd scribbled on the top one. But below that, a paper jutted out with a great deal more written on it. Lines of a script. Stage directions.

Lydia's heart skipped a beat. She whirled to stare at him. Still asleep. Still peaceful. The memories of their tryst swirled around her. No wonder he could conjure up such scenes in her imagination and sweep her away into a fairy story. Max Millerson was M. M. Irgrimm, author of her favorite plays of all time. This unassuming man could spin words that touched her deep inside, and she'd had no idea.

Or maybe, some part of her had known all along.

She scrambled into her clothing and fled.

16
ANHUR
god of war

MAX DREW A SLASH through the words *"The Prince and the Fortune Teller."* Too dull. What else could he try?

Seer? Soothsayer? Oracle? Oracle wasn't bad. But did it go with Prince? Not particularly. "Damnation. This is impossible."

Maybe he'd change the hero too. *The Playwright and the Fortune Teller.*

Lydia would snicker at that. Not that he'd told her his identity. Blast. He needed to do that. He also needed to send her a message after last night. He scratched out some ideas on the same piece of paper.

Thank you for coming to me last night. And coming for me. And with me.

No, no, no. Nothing crass. Though he did have to convey how spectacular the night had been and then offer to make arrangements for next time.

I look forward to our next meeting.

Ugh. Boring. God, he hoped she wasn't bored. Or disappointed. He'd had a momentary panic when he'd woken alone. But staying hadn't been an option for her. She'd had to don her disguise and sneak home. He ought to have seen her out instead of letting himself fall asleep. Next time, he would find some way to make that unnecessary. Maybe he could make a pretense of visiting her cousin Jack. It could work, as long as Jack approved of the liaison.

Or maybe Max ought to start formally courting her. Call

during social hours. Bring her flowers. Take her on a drive through Hyde Park. It all sounded rather pleasant, honestly.

~~Dear Miss Weaver~~ ~~Dearest Lydia~~ *My Enchanting Nymph*

A knock sounded at the door and Max hastily shoved the paper beneath the pile of invitations he was supposed to be replying to.

"Come i—"

"Maxwell."

Adolphus Millerson swept into the room without waiting for an introduction. Behind him, the young porter gave a helpless shrug, then scurried away.

Max's mouth fell open, but no words came out. His father never interrupted him at work. It had been the one boundary he respected. Because endangering Max's employment meant no one would be left to beg money from.

"We have a crisis," his father declared.

Max jumped up from his seat, knocking several invitations to the floor.

"What? What's happened? Is it Lizzie? Is someone hurt, or… or worse?"

For once, his father appeared speechless. His brow furrowed and he blinked rapidly. "Hurt?" He rubbed his temple.

"Tell me!" Max blurted. He rushed around the desk. "What's happened? Who's died?"

His father snapped back from whatever confusion had overtaken him. "For heaven's sake, boy, no one's died. Why would you think that? Lizzie is shut up with her paints. This is about the club."

"The club." Max reeled. He'd been interrupted at work for a problem with the club? This situation was out of control. He had to stop it. But how? He didn't think he could seize control of the finances himself. His father wasn't incapacitated in any way. Merely a spendthrift.

"Yes, of course the club. You saw that mess, with those fools shouting about the mummy's curse. Some oaf wrote it up in the paper, and now our attendance is down. Hardly more than a handful of players a night. Even the new glassware hasn't helped."

"Glassware?" What the devil had he done now?

"I ordered all new glassware for the bar, in keeping with the theme. Gold rimmed, with a lovely ring of little hieroglyphics. Very elegant. Shipment arrived a few days ago."

Max nodded, unable to speak. The panic he'd initially felt wasn't resurfacing. Instead, his simmering, long-suppressed fury had begun to rise to the surface. His fingers curled into fists.

"If it doesn't turn around soon I'll have to sell the club," his father lamented. "And you know it's the only thing left."

Max's jaw clenched. Yes. He knew. The whole point of this club was to ensure that the family could continue on comfortably. It was a solid business to replace all the poorly-managed clubs and squandered investments of the past. Max had done his best to make sure the Curiosity Club could run without his father needing to lift a finger. Unfortunately, his father seemed intent on shoving both hands in and turning everything upside down.

"You can wait it out," Max suggested, fighting for an even tone. "The curse talk will die down and people will return. Be frugal for a few months. You might even like it."

His father gave him that confused blink again. Did he not understand the word frugal, or was he simply horrified by it?

"No, no. Can't do that. Creditors to pay, you know. But I know how we can resolve this."

Max pointed at the open door. "Good. Go resolve it. I have work to do."

His father waved a printed card. "I need your assistance. We need to hold another event. Bring in a spiritualist to declare the place fit for business. Lucky, even. Cleanse the whole building of all bad vibes, that sort of thing." He spun the card so Max could read it. "I need your Madame Xyla."

The rage boiled over. "No. Absolutely not. Get out." Max would not drag Lydia back into this. They had moved on from their business relationship. Become something more. He couldn't jeopardize that, not when it had barely begun.

Besides, he had nothing left to offer her. Nothing but himself.

Every muscle in his body went rigid. Christ, what if he asked her to help and then she thought last night was all a ruse? That he was wooing her and pleasuring her as part of some ploy to get her to do his father's bidding? She would despise him.

Never. He could not let that happen.

"This is *your* mess." Max gestured again at the door, and this time the movement was sharp, aggressive. "Leave me out of it and leave her out of it. Now get the hell out of my office."

Adolphus Millerson wasn't a man prone to anger. He made demands often, but Max couldn't remember the last time he'd raised his voice. Now, though, his face turned almost purple and he shouted loud enough to rattle the door.

"How dare you speak to me in such a manner, you insolent brat! Have you forgotten who raised you?"

"Raised me?" Max's nails bit into his palms. "You can't even raise a finger to help anyone but yourself! I have been keeping this family off the streets since I was seventeen years old! I'm only twenty-five. I should still be a youth, looking up to my father and hoping to follow in his footsteps. Instead, I'm the one spending every spare penny I earn to solve problems not of my own making."

Max's father eyed Max's Harris Tweed waistcoat. "You can spare a few pennies if you're earning enough for clothes like that."

Hot, furious tears burned in the corners of Max's eyes. His wardrobe was his one luxury, paid for entirely with his earnings from his playwriting. If he admitted to the second source of income, he would lose his refuge, and his chance to be himself and make something of himself outside of family pressures.

"Get out of my office," Max repeated.

"Selfish, ungrateful whelp," his father spat. "How can you care so little for your family? You'd leave us to starve on the streets while you waste your time and money on your degenerate friends? What would your sisters think of you?"

The words hit like a punch to the gut. A large part of him wanted to shout, "Go ahead and starve!" His older sisters were fine. Far away, with families of their own. But Lizzie had no education, no job skills, no money whatsoever set aside to provide for her, and absolutely no interest in marriage. All she had was Max.

His father must have sensed the fight go out of him, because he placed Madame Xyla's flyer on the desk, face down. Among the services listed on the back of the card was the phrase, "Investigate hauntings and other spiritual disturbances."

He tapped the paper with a finger. "She can do what I need. Bring her in to help us. Then perhaps I will forgive your unseemly outburst." He spun and strode away.

Max returned to his chair and sank into it, putting his head in his hands. He needed to speak to Lydia, but now he had even less of an idea what to say than before. It had to be done, however, and soon. He also needed to have a long talk with Lizzie.

That, at least, was something he could do. He'd write her a message and invite her out to lunch to chat. He pulled out a fresh sheet of paper and picked up his pen.

"Millerson."

There was no knock this time. Huntington Black strode into the room as if he owned not only the office, but the building and perhaps the entire street. Dressed to suit his name and with a long, white scar across his left cheek, the man could have passed for Lucifer, Death, Hades, or any other harbinger of doom.

"We need to have a talk," he said, in his gravelly voice.

Fuck. Fuck. Fuck.

17

HU

god of the power of the spoken word

LYDIA ENTERED THE PARLOR of the Pyne mansion a half-hour late and dripping from a dash through the rain. Despite her bedraggled state, she walked calmly to the sideboard to pour herself a cup of tea.

Conversation among the assembled ladies ground to a halt. Ginny hopped up from her seat and scurried over.

"Lydia, are you well? Tess told us you had some delay with your business that kept you."

Yes, a delay. A self-made delay.

Lydia stared down at the tea, wishing it were something much stronger. Her mind was sluggish today, unable to process things at her usual brisk pace. She'd been slow to assess the morning's clients. Slow to think up appropriate interpretations for her readings. Her fingers had even been slow with the cards. Too much of her mind remained preoccupied with the events of last night.

She could still feel Max's hands on her skin. Hear the sensual murmur of his voice. Her bed had been cold and lonely. Half-a-dozen times she'd caught herself planning where and when they could meet again, imagining his smile and the sparkle in his eyes.

"Please, have a seat," Ginny went on, gesturing toward a plush armchair. "Would you like something to eat with your tea? I can make up a plate for you while you recover."

Recover? God, did she look that much in distress? True, she was a touch… moist. But nothing a few minutes sitting by the fire wouldn't take care of.

"I'm quite well, thank you." Lydia accepted the chair Ginny had offered, scooting it closer to the hearth and shaking out her skirt before she sat. She sipped at her tea, enjoying the pleasure of the warm liquid sliding down her throat and heating her chilled body.

The other women regarded her with skeptical expressions. For a long moment no one spoke, until Connie at last said, "I'm terribly sorry if this is rude, but you've never been late before, and you appear quite flustered. Is something wrong? You know we will help if at all possible."

Three other heads nodded. Lydia stared at them. Had she lost all ability to conceal her inner thoughts? These ladies appeared to be reading her the way she read her clients. Sensing her turmoil.

People see what they want to see.

Lydia's heart thumped in her chest. Her friends noticed what others didn't because they cared. Her outer presentation didn't matter to them, but her state of mind did. If anyone would listen to her troubles and offer genuine support, it was these women.

Could she tell them? The problem was scandalous, without a doubt. Tess, she could tell. Tess was family. But the others?

Lydia took in their concerned frowns. She could trust these women. She only needed to allow herself to do so.

"Yes, I have a problem," she admitted. She took another sip of her tea, composed herself, then stated the matter outright. "My problem is Mr. Maxwell Millerson. I slept with him, but I didn't achieve the desired result."

Constance gasped and a copper glow suffused her light-brown cheeks. Aramina's pale face turned ashen and she fanned herself vigorously.

"He was a disappointing lover?" Tess asked calmly. "That's unfortunate. Though it explains why you seemed melancholy this morning."

"Oh, dear, oh, dear," Aramina fretted. "Was it horrible? Did it hurt? You poor darling. I can't even imagine. To have a man do… things like that to you?" She shuddered.

Connie touched her friend's arm comfortingly. "It doesn't have to be awful, dear. Sir Nigel is very gentle." Her blush deepened.

Lydia didn't know Constance's husband well. He was a calm, quiet man who had received a knighthood for his engineering work with farm equipment and factory safety. Lydia imagined he and Connie would be sweet and conventional in bed. But one never could tell.

"No one hurt me," Lydia corrected. "That's not the problem. It was delightful." Better than delightful. Sensational. Bone-melting. Her tea was suddenly much too warm and the fire far too close.

"Oh." Tess reclined in her seat, a smug smile playing across her lips. "Now I see. This *is* interesting. Jack was right, it seems."

Ginny had her notebook out and pencil poised. She looked back and forth between Lydia and Tess. "Right about what?"

Tess hesitated, but Lydia waved a hand to give her permission to continue. She couldn't have anything worse to say than Lydia might say herself. And her explanation would tell Lydia whether she had to give her cousin a gentle scolding or throw him into the Thames.

"Lydia has fallen for the son of her sworn enemy," Tess stated succinctly.

Aramina's fan continued to flutter. "How very gothic! He seduced you, then? Like a villain in a novel?"

Lydia tossed back the rest of her tea and looked around the room, hoping to spot a brandy decanter. She found only teapots and plates of small sandwiches. Damn.

"It was a mutually agreed upon tryst of a friendly nature," she corrected. And now she'd admitted aloud that she and Max were friends. Well, it couldn't be denied, she supposed. "It went very well and was highly satisfactory to both parties,

I believe. But it has not diminished my attraction to him, as I had hoped. I find myself instead plagued with thoughts of seeing him again."

There. As uncomfortable as it was begging others for assistance, her words did have a rejuvenating effect. She felt lighter, her muscles more relaxed.

"Because you've fallen for him," Tess reiterated. "Haven't you?"

Lydia couldn't answer. She couldn't deny she felt something for Max. But fallen? No. Fall*ing*. She was falling for him. It wasn't too late to stop the train before it crashed. One way or another, she would overcome this obstacle.

Ginny tapped her pencil against the notebook. "It's peculiar to spend a meeting discussing men, but this does raise some important points. Many women will need to deal with feelings of romance and attraction. Courtship and marriage are common. Women who choose neither may still desire physical relations with men. Love and lust play an important role in the lives of many women and should not be overlooked when considering a woman's path to a full, independent life." She jotted something on the paper. "As for your particular situation, Lydia, I would suggest that you have a talk with your lover. Communication is vital for any relationship. I hope that whatever happens you will be most happy."

"I agree," Tess said. "Talk to him. Leaving feelings unacknowledged won't help. You'll end up flinging yourself onto a boat to New York like Jack did."

Aramina's fan finally slowed. "Polite conversation solves everything."

Lydia rose to fetch more tea. Wonderful. She'd been given an assignment. It sounded oh, so simple. She could walk up to Max and say, "I find myself caring about you rather too much. Oh, and by the way, I'm planning to ruin your father."

She needed brandy.

Madame Xyla guided her seance guests to the door, seeing them off with quiet thanks and slight nods farewell. Few of the dozen guests looked at her for more than a second or two. Their preoccupation was with one another, busily recounting the evening's event. As they glided out the front door, a lone figure approached the house.

Max? Lydia stiffened at the sight of him. What was he doing coming to her house at this time of night?

Her heart fluttered in her chest as he deftly slipped into the hall between clusters of departing guests. Smooth. Calculated. Perhaps he'd come for a repeat of last night's activities. Making good on his offer to be the one doing the sneaking.

The two ladies and one gentleman remaining from the seance appeared not to notice that Max wasn't one of their number.

"Dear Madame Xyla, I cannot thank you enough," one of the ladies gushed. "This was the most enlightening event, and I truly feel more in touch with my metaphysical nature."

Lydia inclined her head. She'd said nothing about metaphysical natures during the seance, but she'd long ago learned that people took what they wanted from her performances. Often times their interpretations of her actions were nothing like what she herself had imagined.

"I'm so glad you enjoyed our session," she said. "Please let me know if I can ever be of service in the future."

The trio departed, leaving only Max behind. Lydia checked that the group wasn't looking back, then closed the door.

She turned to Max, maintaining her aloof Madame Xyla persona. "Mr. Millerson. This is a surprise."

His fingers kneaded the brim of his hat. Nervous again, almost as he had been the first time they'd met. "I'm sorry for appearing without warning. Do you have a moment to talk?"

Lydia's gut clenched.

He's leaving you. Last night was enough for him and now he's not interested. He's come to break it off.

She kept her breathing even, calming the ridiculous worry. So what if he was here to break it off? Wouldn't that be the best option? She couldn't do it herself, apparently, so maybe this was precisely what she needed.

"Work is finished for the evening," she said. "We can talk in the seance room."

Max hung his hat and overcoat in the hall, then followed her into the seance room, closing the door behind him. His eyes tracked across the room, lingering on the curtains covering the walls in strategic locations.

"You've made some changes." His gaze fell to the table, which now sat near a wall rather than in the center of the room.

"Renovation is in progress," Lydia explained. She pulled aside one of the draperies to reveal the open wall and exposed piping. "The new lighting system. I now have my own small version of a gas table, there beside my chair."

"Ah. Yes. Of course." He peered in that direction, but didn't walk closer. Instead, he slid his hands into his pockets.

"You seem nervous," Lydia observed. No sense in letting things linger. Her friends had advised her to talk to him. So she would. "Is there a problem?"

A chill stole over her. He would say he was done with her. They would never relive that magical moment in his bedroom.

"Several problems, I'm afraid," Max replied. "But one of them involves you. Or *could* involve you, rather. I'd prefer it didn't."

The words stabbed into her gut. This was it.

The sting will pass, she told herself. *You'll feel better when it's done.*

"I'm sorry. I'm being unclear," Max continued. "I'm still trying to wrap my head around everything that's happened today. My father is having issues with the club again."

The club? Some of the tension inside Lydia eased, replaced with a jolt of elation. Had the curse worked?

"Because of the mummy?" she asked.

Max nodded. "Apparently the talk of a curse is keeping people away from the club. His ridiculous Egyptian theme only adds to the trouble, I'm sure. He believes the only solution is to perform a spiritual cleansing of the entire building."

"So you need me."

It had worked. Her scheme had truly worked, and now here it was, her opportunity to destroy Adolphus Millerson once and for all. She would declare his club beyond salvation, unfit for business. Then he would either sit and watch it wither to nothing, or he would sell it for pennies. He would be broke within a month.

Guilt knotted in her stomach. *And what will happen to Max?*

Max blew out a heavy breath. "No. I don't need you. My father needs you. He wants me to bring you to the club to dispel the mummy's curse or some such nonsense." He pulled his right hand from his pocket and ran it through his dark hair. "I can't ask you to do that. I can't keep going along with my father's ridiculous whims. I'm sick of the entire thing. And even if I did plan to beg you for this favor, I have nothing left to offer you. I have to do something, but I won't abuse our friendship in this way."

Lydia took a step toward him, her heart lightening more with every word he spoke. She didn't need to worry what might happen to Max. He'd be better off for this. In one blow she would destroy his father and free him from his burdens.

"I'm happy to help," she told him.

Max's eyes widened. "You are? But... there's no obligation. I only wanted to warn you that my father may insist upon you doing this. He may—I don't know—blame you for the curse, perhaps?"

She waved a hand. "It doesn't matter. I'll accept his offer to hold a spiritual event."

Max continued to stare at her. "And the part where I have nothing to give you in return? I can't imagine my father does, either."

One corner of Lydia's mouth twitched upward. "Traditionally, this is where you pledge to give me your first-born child."

The worried lines in his brow smoothed out as he smiled. "Now you're teasing me."

"I don't tease."

His smile grew. "Yes, you do. You like to pretend you're always serious, but I know better. Fun, playful Lydia is as much you as practical Lydia or Madame Xyla Lydia. She loves stories of adventure and romance. She likes to swordfight. She is a nymph in the moonlight. Just because she is shy of the world doesn't mean she doesn't exist." He turned to look at her seance table again, and the knobs jutting from the wall that controlled her lights. "You think stage lighting is all Practical Lydia? I don't think so. I think it's Fun Lydia."

He wasn't wrong. In fact, he was far too right. Lydia didn't understand how he managed to coax those parts of her into the open. Fun was usually a brief indulgence on her own. A show at the theater or a book in her room at night. Outside of occasional antics with Jack, it wasn't a side of herself she cared to share.

There was something about Max, though. Something about the way he saw her, despite the costumes she wore or the roles she played. It tugged at her heart. It was why she was falling.

"Would you like a demonstration of the new lights?" she asked. And there she went, tumbling further, when she ought to be sending him away.

"Yes, please."

Lydia walked to her controls and turned the knob to lower the main lights. "This is the general room lighting. On for most basic consultations, off for a seance. Then we have the smaller wall sconces." She turned off the main lights completely and turned another knob, bathing the room in a fainter glow from the new lamps.

"I like the mirrored cages surrounding the lamps," Max remarked. "They give the impression of antique lanterns hung on the wall."

"I think so too. It's a good atmosphere for a reading or event that doesn't require bright light. This last one is my favorite, though." Again, she closed one valve and opened another. This time, a shaft of silvery-blue light shone down from her special colored lamp to cast a shimmering circle in the center of her table.

"Moonlight," Max whispered, his voice dropping into the same soft caress that had entranced her the night before.

"Yes." Lydia walked around the table to stand next to him. She placed her hand palm down in the circle of light. "I can lay out the cards here."

His fingers grazed her hip. When she didn't pull away, he lifted his other hand and grasped her waist. "I'm sure the cards look lovely in the moonlight."

"They do." Lydia raised her hand from the table and placed it against his chest, her fingers skimming beneath the edge of his waistcoat.

Falling. Falling. How did she stop this?

"But it's not the cards that belong in the moonlight." Max leaned over her, his eyes afire in the dim light. In one smooth motion, he lifted her off the floor and set her on the edge of the table. The light pooled around her, casting reflections and shadows across her body and clothing.

"You," he breathed. "You belong here."

Lydia's pulse raced. She couldn't stop it. The hill was too steep. Or perhaps it wasn't a hill at all, but a cliff. She twined her arms around Max's neck, pressed her lips to his, and stepped off the edge.

18
NUT

goddess of the sky, stars, and the cosmos

H_{E HADN'T COME HERE} with seduction in mind.

Max swirled his tongue into Lydia's mouth, tumbling into the taste of her while her fingers tangled in his hair.

No. Correction. He *had* come here with seduction in mind, but it hadn't been his intention. It had been a distant fantasy. An if-only. He had planned to apprise her of the situation, make his apologies, and leave.

He nudged her knees apart, fitting himself between her legs, until the juncture of her thighs came up flush against his rapidly stiffening cock.

Leave? What a ridiculous notion. Why in heaven's name would he ever have considered leaving?

Finally, *finally* he'd found something good in this unholy mess of a day. His father hovered on the brink of ruin. Lizzie's future was at stake. Max was one wrong word from losing his job.

But at least he had this. He had Lydia.

He slowly broke the kiss, dragging his mouth away and giving a gentle suck on her bottom lip as he let it slide from between his.

Moving with languid deliberation, he ground against her as his eyes drank her in. A flush to her cheeks. Wide eyes. A slight arch to her back as she rubbed her sex along his.

God, she was beautiful. In her seance garb, she was bedecked with gold. Her lips were a bright red, done in a quality lip paint that didn't smear when he kissed her. Her lashes were dark, and a wig of brunette curls framed her face. Different than her usual look, and yet very much the same. Very much *her*.

Max gripped the smooth fabric of her skirt and pushed it upward, running his hands over her calves to her bare thighs. She shifted, helping him move the fabric aside.

"Lydia," he groaned. "I've been thinking of you all day. Craving you."

"Yes," she gasped. She hitched her skirts even higher, parted the fabric of her drawers, and stroked herself. "Yes, Max. I'm ready. I want you."

He didn't have to be told twice. Fumbling frantically, he unfastened his trousers and positioned himself at her entrance. Her arms encircled him, tugging him closer, urging him to drive into her. They both moaned as their bodies joined.

She was bliss. Hot, wet, sheer bliss.

Max pressed his lips to her neck. "If I were a god," he rasped. "I would be the moon, so I could be above you every night. See you shimmering beneath me."

He'd clearly been reading too much ancient mythology of late. Everything was gods and moons and poetic imagery. But Lydia seemed to like it, considering the way she pressed into each of his thrusts.

"Oh, Max," she sighed. Her movements became more urgent, spurring him to thrust harder, faster. "I love your words."

She may as well have said, "I love *you*," for that was the way his foolish heart responded to it. It gave a wild, frenetic leap of joy. Again and again he pounded into her, drowning in her siren's song, desperate to claim some small part of this incomparable, unobtainable woman.

"My goddess," he breathed. "I worship you on your midnight altar."

And then the words could no longer form. A tingle began

at the base of his spine. He squeezed his eyes shut, fighting the onrushing climax, straining to make this last as long as possible.

Lydia, too, was close. Her breath quickened and her body tensed, her grip tightening on him.

Yes, darling, Max begged silently. *Come for me. Please, come for me. I can't hold on.*

She shuddered and cried out, clutching him as the orgasm swept her away. The exquisite sensation of her body tightening around him catapulted Max over the edge. White hot bliss speared through him, and he jerked free of her, spilling on her thigh.

Gasping, he sagged against her. Her head fell on his shoulder. For a long moment, they remained there, clinging to one another.

"I don't know what you paid for that light," he said, turning his head to press a kiss to her temple. "But it was worth every penny."

Lydia's laugh shook her entire body. "How do you do it?" she wondered. "How do you make the ordinary so very extraordinary?"

He didn't. It was her. All her. She made the whole world seem a stage—a place of magic, where anything could happen. When Max was with her, whether at a gaming club or in a seance room, he felt free to be himself. Free to let his imagination run wild.

Unfortunately, that imagination was now conjuring up fairy tale endings and true love's kisses. He was deeply, dangerously infatuated.

He held her tight against him, breathing in her scent, tasting her soft skin. "When can I see you again?"

"I..." She stiffened. "I don't know."

Max relaxed his grip and eased away from her, tugging her skirts down before setting himself to rights. "I ought to be getting home. But I would love to see you tomorrow, if possible.

You are welcome to come to my flat, or I can arrange to come here again. Or neutral ground, if you prefer. An abandoned warehouse. A secluded garden. A nice hotel."

Lydia was the one who had the most to lose if this affair became public knowledge. The decision was hers to make. But Max wanted her to have as many options as possible.

"I'll give it some thought," she replied.

Not the enthusiastic reply he might have liked, but not a rejection. Max responded with a slight nod. She could take whatever time she needed to decide.

"And as for the club," he said, suddenly remembering the reason he'd come here in the first place. "Please do not feel obligated…"

She raised a hand to halt him. "I'll handle your father."

The unwavering confidence in her voice had Max envisioning her sweeping into his father's office to read him the riot act. She would demand he change his ways, stop endangering the family, and never beg Max for money again.

Another ridiculous fantasy. She was going to the club as a spiritualist. To perform a cleansing of the curse or whatnot. She was not riding in on a white horse to play knight to Max's damsel.

She wasn't doing this for him at all. It was a smart business move, most likely. The event would be written up in the papers. She'd earn more clients. And that was as it should be. They were only recently friends. Barely lovers. It was foolish to expect more than mild affection and excellent physical compatibility.

But, damn, did Max wish it were more.

"Thank you for inviting me in," he said. "You never cease to astound me." He leaned in for a goodbye kiss, soft and lingering.

"Thank you for coming," she replied, when they separated again. "I had a lovely time."

Lydia slid off the table at last and walked over to her lighting controls, turning the moonbeam off and the main lights on. The room was an ordinary room again, but Max's fevered imagination did not dim. She remained his princess and he would slay monsters to win her.

After a brief farewell and a second lengthy goodbye kiss, Max ducked out into the cool night air and started for home. He tilted his head back to feel the drizzle on his face, sharp and cold. Invigorating. In the real world, he had no monsters to slay, and he was far from a prince. But fair lady could still be won. Starting tomorrow, he would woo her, to the very best of his ability. Which meant wielding his finest weapon. His pen.

19
NEFERTUM
god of the lotus flower

A SINGLE FLOWER ARRIVED with the morning post. Lydia lifted it carefully from atop the small pile of papers. It was a bright, delicate thing, pale pink, with darker tips on every petal. A small paper tag had been tied to it with a bit of twine. She flipped it over to read the words written on the other side.

"Aha! He's sending you flowers at last," Jack crowed from the opposite side of the breakfast table. "I knew he was smitten!" He took a large bite of bacon, then tossed a smaller bit at Phantom, who perched nearby.

"Care to share what the note says?" Tess asked. She wiped a bit of porridge from Alexandria's face. The little girl looked to have more of her food on her face and hands than in her belly.

"No, I don't particularly care to share," Lydia replied. "But you are my family, so I suppose you ought to know what is happening in my life."

Tess glanced at her husband. "She means there's no point in hiding it, because you'd only steal it and read it."

Jack fed another morsel to the cat, then scratched her behind the ears. "My own wife thinks I'm a scoundrel."

Of course she did. Tess hid it well, but the people who knew her knew she craved adventure and liked to break rules. Jack's rascally but good-hearted nature suited her perfectly.

Lydia twirled the flower in her fingers. For years she'd been telling herself she was content to be a spinster. And for the most part, it was true. She'd always had Jack, so she'd never lacked for a deep, abiding bond with another person. But watching him fall in love had altered something in her. They didn't have to be alone, just the two of them.

Jack's marriage hadn't lessened his connection with Lydia, even across an ocean. Circumstances had changed, but she hadn't lost him. And she'd gained Tess and Alex.

Maybe she could do the same. Allow herself to reach out. Form more bonds, the way Jack had.

But, then again, Jack was warm and friendly. Lydia was neither.

She examined her note, taking in the smooth pen strokes and the neatly-formed letters. Max had taken his time writing this, unlike the scrawled notes she'd seen at his bedside.

"It's nothing scandalous or remarkable," she told the others. "It merely says, 'The rose is red, the violet's blue. My thoughts are filled with naught but you.' Sweet, but not extraordinary."

"Clever, though," Tess replied.

"Oh?"

"That's a pansy." Tess pointed at the flower. "In flower language it's symbolic of thoughts. The note is expressly stating that the flower was chosen with intent. I expect it will be the first of many such gifts."

Lydia's knowledge of the language of flowers began and ended with "rose = love." She liked flowers, and many beautiful embroidered ones adorned the gowns and turbans she wore as Madame Xyla. She'd never thought beyond the colors and shapes, however. Apparently, she would need to remedy that.

After attending to her morning clients, Lydia went for her usual walk, detouring to the bookstore. Upon her return, she discovered that her purchase of *An Illustrated Guide to Flowers and Their Language* had been wise indeed. Another single flower awaited her, accompanied by a longer note than the first.

Lydia combed the book for the yellow, swirly-petaled flower. She nearly missed it, as the example in the illustration was pink, but listed beneath were alternate colors, including white and yellow. Ranunculus.

Below the identification was the symbolic meaning: You are radiant with charms.

"Radiant with charms?" she wondered aloud, unfolding the note. Max was the charming one, if you asked her. She began to read.

> *There once was a nymph 'neath the moon,*
> *Whose charms made a poor young man swoon.*
> *He had so much fun,*
> *That when they were done,*
> *He begged her to come again soon.*

Lydia's laugh was so abrupt it came out as a snort. Not only charming, but funny and wicked, apparently. Damn the man. Once again he was distracting her from her purpose. She ought to be planning for the event that would see Adolphus Millerson forever ruined. Everything had to be done carefully. The club needed to fold. And she needed to make people believe—without stating outright—that Millerson was at fault. No one would step in to loan him money or salvage anything if they believed he tainted everything he touched. And honestly, it wasn't far from the truth.

Lydia turned back to her note, thoughts of Max once again blotting out those of his father.

Meet me at the theater tonight? the note continued. *You said you loved* Scarlet and the Wolf, *and I'd love to watch it with you.*

Her heart gave a wild leap. *His* play. What would it be like to see it again, knowing it had sprung from his imagination? Seeing his reactions to it?

It would be glorious. She could picture his smile, hear his laugh. Her whole body warmed at the image in her mind. She would lean close to him, whisper her questions. Perhaps sneak a kiss in the dark.

"Enjoying your letter?" Jack's teasing voice called.

Lydia jumped. She hadn't even noticed him enter the hall,

but there he stood, his daughter propped on one hip. Lydia scowled at him.

He held up his free hand in a gesture of innocence. "I didn't read it."

"And you never will," she vowed.

Jack's mouth curved. "That good, eh?"

"I will be going to the theater after my evening appointments," Lydia declared. "In return for abandoning you tonight, I'll buy you two tickets for another performance. I'll mind Alex and you and Tess can have a night out."

Jack's eyes lit up. He strode over to plant a kiss on her cheek. "Thank you, darling. That's so thoughtful of you." His impish grin reappeared. "I hope you have a fabulous time tonight. Don't stay out all night. I don't duel, so the only solution would be for you to marry the chap. Or do stay out all night, if that's what you want."

Lydia swept past him, ignoring the teasing. She didn't even know what she wanted anymore. That was the problem.

The Enchantment Theatre. The name fit. Tonight the whole street dazzled beneath the gas lamps, ringing with the laughter of the mingling ladies and gentlemen in their finest garb. A pleasantly warm night kept people outside, lingering in front of the doors to greet friends. Somewhere in this vibrant throng Max awaited her.

An upper-class lady in a lavender silk dress wafted past Lydia, catching her eye for an instant before continuing on into the theater. One of Madame Xyla's clients from earlier today. Had the woman recognized her?

Lydia reached up to ensure that her turban was securely tied, suddenly uncertain about her fashion choices. She'd worn a simple, but elegant dress in a pale blue. The sort she usually wore for an evening out. But the turban was one she ordinarily reserved for her spiritualist sessions: gold, with enormous flowers embroidered on one side. She'd picked it for the symbolic meaning. To show Max she'd understood his messages. Naturally, she'd had to accessorize to match. Her lip paint was the same vibrant red as the flowers on her turban, and her earrings were large gold dangles. A necklace of stacked gold chains with pale blue beads tied the entire outfit together. She'd loved the look when she'd dressed, but now…

Was she still unobtrusive Lydia Weaver? Would people recognize her as Madame Xyla? Or would they simply be confused?

"Lydia!" Max zigzagged through the crowd toward her, his eyes shining with delight. "You came!"

"I did." she replied when he reached her side. "Thank you for the invitation."

"My pleasure. You look radiant tonight."

"Radiant with charms," she agreed.

Max laughed. "I see you decoded the flowers."

"I bought a book."

"A woman after my own heart." He crooked his arm. "Shall we?"

She took his arm, that tiny touch igniting wild flames of longing inside her. The words "my own heart" echoed in her ears. Why did she want him so damned badly? And not only in her bed. She wanted to claim his heart. To declare to the world that this man with his smart words and his sweet flowers was hers and hers alone. She never should have flung herself at him last night. Or accepted this invitation.

This is not only about desire, Lydia told herself. *It's a sensible business decision. He'll take you backstage after the show and you can chat with the cast and crew. You'll need assistants to complete your revenge. You can recruit some here.*

"I have one more flower for you today," Max declared as he led her into the building. He touched the cluster of tiny purple blooms pinned to his lapel. "Vervain. Enchantment."

"The perfect choice for a night at this theater." Lydia

couldn't stop a grin from spreading across her face. "You are a true lover of wordplay, Mr. Millerson. I can see it in everything you write."

His brows knit together. "The notes?"

"And your plays."

Max flinched. His gaze darted all around, as if looking to see whether anyone had heard. He quickened his pace and didn't reply until they'd reached their seats.

"You know who I am?" he whispered, bending close as they lowered themselves onto the cushions.

"I do. I saw your play-in-progress on your bedside table. I'm sorry for mentioning it. You wouldn't want to be suddenly mobbed by people."

He gave a small huff. "I doubt that would happen. But I would prefer word not get back to my father."

Lydia's jaw tightened. If she didn't have enough reason to hate Adolphus Millerson, here was something else to add. The bastard would never leave Max alone if he knew. He would do all he could to take advantage of even a hint of celebrity status. She would enjoy taking him down.

"I'll keep your secret," she promised. "Although I think I may be revealing my own tonight."

He frowned in puzzlement. "What do you mean?"

"All this." She waved a hand over her upper half and flicked one of her earrings, setting it swaying. "Do I look too much like Madame Xyla tonight?"

"You look like you. It would never have occurred to me to think anything else. And so what if someone recognizes you? Spiritualists are people. They're allowed to have a life outside the seance room."

Lydia had never considered Madame Xyla outside the seance room. She played the role for her work. But the spiritualist didn't exist outside that sphere. Did she?

"But if it's a problem," Max continued, "I will swear up and down that you couldn't possibly be Madame Xyla to anyone who asks."

Lydia laughed. "That's very kind of you, but unnecessary. I think I can slip into the role if need be." She shifted in her seat, bringing her shoulder up against his. "I'm more interested in *your* alter ego," she whispered. "I want you to tell me all the secrets behind this show."

"I'd be happy to."

Other patrons filtered into the seats all around them, and soon enough the lights turned down. Having seen backstage and learned about the lighting gave Lydia a new appreciation for the mechanics of the show, and she found herself giving more thought to those aspects of the play than she had when she'd seen it before. *Scarlet and the Wolf* was a marvel of collaboration. Max's words, the actors' performances, and the crew's scene setting all combined to create an immersive spectacle. Lydia found herself sucked in, despite knowing both the story and many of the tricks behind the production.

Throughout the show, Max pressed close, whispering little tidbits in her ear. Here was where an actor changed a few words to fit his interpretation of the character. There was where the costume designer turned the phrase "dressed all in red" into a stunning crimson gown that had the audience joining Wolf in his wonderment at the sight of Scarlet.

When he wasn't murmuring secrets into her ear, Max was laughing alongside her. He smiled when she did, blushed when she praised her favorite parts, and gave his friends onstage enthusiastic cheers whenever appropriate. Never had Lydia enjoyed the theater more.

When the cast began their final bows, a pang of sadness struck Lydia's heart. She didn't want this to end. This was a place of happiness. Of shared joys and whispered secrets. The idea of going backstage and recruiting actors to join her revenge spectacle no longer appealed. To be completely honest, she didn't want to go backstage at all. She didn't want anyone else to intrude on her time with Max.

Dammit, dammit, what have I done?

"I trust you enjoyed the show?" he asked, a touch of pink still coloring his cheeks. Was he flustered by her enthusiasm for his work, or was that a flush of desire tinting his skin? Both, perhaps.

"I loved it," she answered truthfully. "Thank you so much for inviting me."

His reply was low and husky. "It was absolutely my pleasure. Shall I walk you home?"

Words fell from her mouth before she could think them through. "Your flat is closer."

His hand closed over hers, giving a possessive squeeze. "Very true."

They were both eager tonight, shedding clothes as rapidly as possible the moment they stepped through his door. But when their bodies met, every touch was tender, every kiss reverent. Max worshiped her, slowly and thoroughly, until Lydia couldn't stand it any longer, and she flipped him onto his back and rode him until they were both exhausted.

Some indeterminate amount of time later, she jerked awake in his arms. Bloody hell, she'd actually fallen asleep. Thank God she hadn't slept until morning. She needed to get up, dress, and hurry home at once.

Her body remained still.

Get up, she scolded herself.

She didn't move.

Go on. Get up.

Her eyes remained locked on her lover, so peaceful and content. So warm and cozy.

Lydia couldn't make herself get out of bed, but she did manage to roll over. Enough to see his pile of notes at the bedside table, illuminated by the streetlamp outside the window. The limerick from her note smiled up at her—a first draft with bits crossed out and edited. Beneath it, slightly askew, was what appeared to be the beginning of a play. The words, "The Prince and the Fortune Teller," had been written neatly at the top. A bold stroke sliced through the word "Prince." Above it, scrawled at an angle, Max had written, "Scribe."

Her heart spasmed.

Max's pull on her was so much more than "warm and cozy." He was sweet and funny. Clever and observant. Gentle. Kind. Perfect.

She loved him. She genuinely, truly loved him, and she didn't want to leave. Not now, not ever.

Jack's earlier words taunted her. *The only solution would be for you to marry the chap.*

Lydia pushed herself up out of the bed and snatched up her clothing. It was time to return home. She couldn't entertain any thoughts of the future until she had her revenge completed, and she'd freed Max from his tyrannical father. Only then would she have time to sift through these strange new feelings besieging her heart.

Before she left, she pressed a kiss to Max's cheek. "Sleep well, darling."

He stirred at her words. "Night, love," he mumbled.

Tell him, urged some voice in the back of her mind. *Tell him you love him. Tell him your plans. Tell him everything in your heart.*

Lydia turned and walked out the door.

20
RENENUTET
goddess of fortune and prosperity

MAX FINISHED OFF ANOTHER tedious letter and set it aside in the pile awaiting Mr. Black's signature. Yes, the man was wealthy, but what good did it do him when his entire life was a never-ending stream of work? He never accepted any of the invitations he received, and he worked much longer hours than Max ever had.

Except for the past few days, when Max had nearly matched him.

Be a model employee. Don't get sacked.

Which meant no dawdling in the mornings. No long breaks for lunch. No daydreaming. No working on other projects.

He'd failed at those last two, mostly because of Lydia. This morning he'd sent her a white dittany—a sign of passion—with a short message telling her how much he'd loved their night at the theater. Sharing the secrets behind his work had brought a special kind of joy, and he couldn't wait to do it again. He wanted to share everything with her. Every project, every touch, every smile, every day.

He consulted his list of flower meanings. Was this afternoon a good time for lupine, imagination? Or maybe meadow lychnis for wit. Maybe he ought to simply throw in all his chips and send her a red tulip, a well-known declaration of love.

Whatever he sent, he would be including the first several pages of *The Scribe and the Fortune Teller.*

Max tucked the list away and returned to his work. He had time yet to think on it. He touched pen to paper, but instead of replying to the letter sitting beside him, he began to write a note to his sister. He hadn't talked to Lizzie yet, with the extra time at work foiling his plans for a luncheon together. But perhaps he could stop by the house later, when their father was off at the club.

A knock on the door made his pen skid across the paper, leaving a long black smear. Max grumbled a curse and covered the note with a different paper.

"Come in," he called.

A rosy-cheeked messenger boy bounded into the room and doffed his cap. "Note from yer lady, sir," he declared, presenting a folded piece of paper. "Gave me a whole shilling to bring it right quick!" The lad beamed. "She's a fine lady, she is."

"She absolutely is," Max agreed, accepting the letter. He tossed the boy an extra tuppence. "I'll let you know as soon as I have my next flower delivery ready."

"At yer service, guv." The lad made a sweeping bow and departed.

Max tore into Lydia's message, his pulse racing. He couldn't see her during the day, but seeing her words and imagining them in her voice was infinitely better than any daydream.

Dear Max,

I now entirely understand the appeal of flower language. I find both satisfaction and joy in identifying and decoding each new blossom. The white dittany is most appropriate! I regret that tonight I must stay in, as Jack and Tess will be attending the theater, and I will be minding Alexandria. They are here only a short time longer and I want to be certain they have time to enjoy themselves and I have time to spoil my niece. If you are available tomorrow, however, I would love to see you. I have no evening seance or readings scheduled, so I will have plenty of time if you'd like to have dinner, take in another show, or find another activity. Art gallery? Museum? A cozy fire and books? Ideas welcome.

Affectionately,
Lydia

Oh, Max had ideas. Scores of ideas. He could take her to his favorite pub. They could walk in the park. Hire a carriage to drive them in circles while they made love inside. He could shower her with ideas, and he would. But first, he needed to finish this note to Lizzie and then return to answering Black's dreary correspondence. No, Mr. Black did not wish to invest in your questionable mining venture. Yes, Mr. Black would be happy to donate the usual sum to the foundling hospital.

God, how he despised this job.

"Millerson." Black's low voice sounded from outside the door before it swung open. He strode into the room, a scowl on his face. "Are you using my errand boys to send personal messages?"

Max rocked back in his chair, shocked at the accusation. "Certainly not!"

Black's boys often sat idle for long portions of the day, but Max had gone out of his way to hire a different lad—or so he'd thought. Max had a wandering mind and filled his own spare time with personal writing, but he'd never misused his employer's funds or supplies. He even bought his own pens and ink. Apparently increasing his hours to display his dedication had been for naught. He was an ungrateful, scheming employee no matter what he did.

"I do not have time to spare for your family drama," Black groused. "Nor will I cater to your romantic whims. Play your silly love games on your own time."

The words themselves stabbed, but the condescending tone behind them shoved the blade in all the further. Max was silly.

His fantasies and imaginings were silly. His courtship was silly. Everything he loved, nothing more than silly, boyish games.

He rose abruptly. "I quit."

Max had never seen Huntington Black flustered before, but now his dark brows lifted and his jaw dropped.

"I beg your pardon?"

"I. Quit." Max repeated. "This is over. It's clear you're no longer pleased with my work, and I'm tired of it myself. I will pack up my things and go." He opened the drawer of his desk and began stuffing inkpots and pens into his pockets. His single notebook and a few personal papers he tucked under one arm. "Good day, sir." He walked right past Black and headed for the exit, not looking back.

No more. No more people who didn't appreciate him. No more people who looked down on him for who he was. Max was through living life for others at the expense of himself. As he stepped outside, he took a deep breath. For the first time in many years, he felt truly free.

"I will have your remaining pay sent to you at home," Black's cool voice called after him.

Max nearly faltered in his furious stride. Oh, God. What had he done? He'd thrown away his steady source of income. Who would support the family? What would his freedom cost them? Throwing propriety to the wind, he jogged down the street in the direction of his father's house.

He arrived red-faced and slightly out of breath, but the housekeeper ushered him through the door without questioning his disheveled state. Max tossed his hat and papers on the side table and rushed to Lizzie's studio at the back of the house. This might be the last time he would see her there. They would have to sell this house and hope it brought in enough money for a small cottage in the country and provisions to last until Max found a new job.

As usual, she sat by the large windows, working on her art. Today she was sketching ideas in a notebook. An easel stood nearby, displaying a finished landscape. Her head snapped up when she heard Max enter.

"Max! What a lovely surprise!" She paused, her smile fading to a frown of concern. "Is something wrong? You appear distressed."

"Yes. I'm afraid so." He hurried across the room, and when she held out her hands he took them both in his. "Oh, Lizzie, I'm so sorry. I've made a hash of everything. I quit my position with Mr. Black."

A furrow appeared in her brow. "But I thought you disliked the work. Isn't this what you wanted?"

"Yes, but without the income…"

Her face brightened. "Oh! You have need of money? I can lend you a sum to tide you over."

"No, Lizzie." Max dropped her hands and turned away. "Father has nothing to give me. He's hopeless. I can't keep him solvent any longer. He might save his club temporarily, but in the end he's doomed. He'll lose it. He'll lose everything."

Lizzie let out a sigh of resignation. "I feared as much. You've worked so hard to make things easy for him, but he never does seem to listen to you." She placed a hand on Max's shoulder. "But I didn't mean my pin money. I can lend you *my* money. From my private account."

Max whirled around. His sister smiled up at him, her soft brown eyes wide and affectionate.

"*Your* account?" She had an account? Since when? And how?

"Yes. When my paintings began to sell, I consulted with the other ladies from my artists' salon. They advised me about trusted bankers and the proper handling of my earnings. I hope to someday purchase a residence outside of town with my savings. I have over five hundred pounds thus far."

Max's mouth fell open and stayed that way. She had been selling her art. She had five hundred pounds. Next to her, Max was a pauper. He could hardly comprehend it.

"So, you see?" Lizzie continued. "I have the means to support you for a time. How much do you need?"

"I-I don't need money," Max managed at last. "I have enough to get by. But..." He ran a hand through his hair. "Egad, Lizzie, I thought I was protecting you. I thought you needed me. And all this time..."

"That's very sweet of you, but I am a fully grown woman and two years your senior."

"I know, but..." He couldn't think of anything to say that wouldn't sound foolish. Because it was. Because he'd been a fool.

"But I'm a woman," she huffed.

"No. I know plenty of competent women. But Father always sheltered you and never educated you on anything practical, such as finances."

"Which doesn't mean I can't learn on my own. My mind is not *always* on my art."

"Clearly. I'm sorry. I underestimated you. Badly. Unforgivably."

Lizzie laughed. "Nonsense. I forgive you already. I ought to have at least mentioned that I was selling my art. I thought it best if Papa didn't know."

"Wise."

Her smile was gentle. "You're certain you're well, then? In truth, I think you've underestimated yourself, too. You've wanted to leave that job for years, but you always seemed to think you couldn't. Now you have. Congratulations."

The last vestiges of Max's panic subsided, and once again the feeling of freedom swept over him. He could pursue his passions. Write more. Perhaps get a position at the theater. He could take some of the stage managing tasks from Irv, who would prefer to be acting anyhow. Or work on advertisements. Writing catchy slogans would be fun.

"I'm done supporting Father," he told Lizzie. "I'm willing

to help him move to the country for a quiet retirement, but nothing further."

She nodded. "I agree. It's time he handled his own problems."

"Thank you." Max kissed her cheek. "Thank you for everything, and I'm so sorry for not seeing how well you were on your own. I suppose I always wanted to play knight in shining armor. But I don't make a very good hero."

Lizzie kissed him back. "Yes, you do. Not all heroes wear armor. Some fight with their heart."

It was as if she'd materialized out of the mist and given him a quest. Max's entire body jolted with sudden awareness of what to do. He could fight with his heart, and he had something to fight for.

His relationship with Lydia had the potential to be truly spectacular. Nothing would hold him back now. He would devote more time to her. Plan a future where he wouldn't be a burden, begging for help, but a partner. Where she eased his worries and he led her into the moonlight, where she could shine.

But first, he would tell her exactly how fierce a grip she had on his heart.

"I have to go," he blurted. He gave his sister a bow. Every knight could use a magical guide like her. "Thank you, Lizzie. Thank you so very much. I love you."

"I love you, too. Oh, and Max?" she called as he scampered from the room.

"Yes?"

"You must bring your lady here to meet me."

Max chuckled to himself as he rushed away. Damn. Lizzie knew everything. Maybe she *did* have magic.

21
HATHOR
goddess of love

Lʏᴅɪᴀ ᴛᴡɪsᴛᴇᴅ ʜᴇʀ ʙʀᴀᴄᴇʟᴇᴛs around and around as she stared down at her notes. She had to get this right. Much of the plan was finished. She knew exactly where she would position herself, Adolphus Millerson, her confederates, and her audience. Both the sphinx fountain and the secret passage in the hall upstairs would serve a purpose.

The words, though. The words were perhaps the most important piece of this puzzle, and she couldn't get them right.

She paused to take another bite of the sweet, succulent peach Max had sent her this morning. Lydia chewed slowly, savoring the flavor, before setting the remaining half of the fruit down in the dainty porcelain dish decorated with pineapples.

Max's note sat beside it.

A real pineapple was too expensive, but I hope this will convey the same sentiment.

When Lydia had received it, she'd raced to consult her book, discovering that the pineapple meant, "You are perfect," and the peach meant, "Your qualities, like your charms, are unequalled." Now every bite of the delicious fruit made her heart sing with love.

She needed to make her plan work for him. And not merely by ruining his detestable father. Which put her right back to fretting about her script. It wouldn't do to have an eerie voice moaning, "You, Adolphus Millerson, are at fault! You must turn over your club to your son at once and never return!"

Yet that was the sentiment she must convey. Everyone in

attendance needed to leave believing that Adolphus was the cursed party and ownership of the club must fall to Max.

Lydia doubted Max wanted the club, but after this he would be able to sell it for a fair price, confident that his father would no longer have the means to waste the money.

Her only problem was choosing the right words.

"Max would be so much better at this," she grumbled. What this plan needed was a dose of his wit and creativity. Unfortunately, asking him would require telling him everything.

Lydia's fingers clenched. She couldn't. When the event was over, he would understand. Afterward, when he saw how she had freed him from his father's grasp, he'd be willing to listen. He would know she did care for him, regardless of how her scheme had begun.

The whistle of the doorbell made her jump. Who would be calling at this time of day? All her appointments had concluded. Jack and Tess had taken Alex out for an afternoon at the park. Max would be working.

Lydia gathered her notes into a neat stack, then walked to the front door to meet her mystery caller. She found Max standing on her porch, a nervous smile on his face and one hand behind his back.

"Max!" Happiness spread through her at the sight of him. "This is a pleasant surprise."

"Miss Weaver." He doffed his hat. "May I beg a moment of your time?"

"Please. Come in."

He stepped through the door before revealing what he held behind him: a single red tulip. He presented it to her with a bow. "Personal delivery today."

Lydia accepted the bloom with trembling fingers. Without her book at hand, she couldn't give the flower a definite meaning, but she knew what the color red represented. This was a love token.

"Not working today?" she asked, using her smooth Madame Xyla voice to conceal her unease.

"I have left my position with Mr. Black," Max replied. "I'm intending to work at the theater, if they'll have me, and use my time to write more. I'm thinking of a series of 'twisted tragedies' where I turn sad endings upside down." His smile turned bashful. "I hope you don't mind a temporarily unemployed suitor."

Lydia lifted the tulip to her nose and inhaled its subtle scent. "I was never attracted to you for your money."

That drew a chuckle from him. "Thank God for that."

Max began to fidget, so Lydia waved a hand at the seance room. "Shall we sit? Would you like tea?"

"No tea, thank you. But, yes, let's sit. I… have things I should like to say to you."

Lydia led the way into the seance room, where she selected a pair of chairs by the window. She pulled the drapes back to let in the sunlight before she sat.

"So, what did—" she began.

"You look l—" Max broke off with a flush when he realized he'd talked over her. "I beg your pardon."

"No, please continue. I should like to hear your dire pronouncement."

"Dire?"

She grinned at him. "You are clearly nervous, so it must be. Or were you saying that I look lovely?"

"Very lovely." His expression relaxed into a smile. As he looked her up and down, the smile grew hotter. Hunger sparked in his light-brown eyes. "This ensemble suits you well."

"Does it?"

"Absolutely."

Lydia's cheeks warmed with pleasure. Everything she'd chosen today had been for herself. The pale green dress was cheerful, but sensible. She'd worn the bracelets on her wrist because she liked the musical sound when they clinked together.

The vibrant purple turban embroidered with pink roses showed she was still celebrating Max's flower game. And her lip paint was a shade she believed made her lips look kissable.

None of it was meant to play a particular role or to make people think certain things about her. It was simply what had struck her fancy. And she might never have dressed this way if Max hadn't encouraged her to be however she liked, whenever she liked.

Her pulse quickened. She held her tulip carefully with the tips of her fingers so as not to accidentally crush it. She hadn't been wrong the other night, believing she loved him. This wasn't lust, nor was it friendship, though it included both. And she had no earthly idea how to handle it.

She fluttered her eyelashes at him. Flirting, she knew. "I can wear anything at all and you like it, don't you? Or perhaps nothing?"

"I do enjoy your naked nymph look." Max gave her a wicked grin, but quickly sobered. "But it is only one of many. I like your simple, sensible look. I like your spiritualist look. I even like you in that ugly dress you use for your flirtatious prostitute disguise. I enjoy seeing all the different Lydias."

"They're only roles I play." Lydia twisted her bracelets. Was this a role she was playing as well? If so, it was an unfamiliar one.

"I don't think they are," Max argued. "Naturally, you present yourself differently to different people. We all do. But you *are* flirty and fun Lydia, who brazenly trounces men at cards and enjoys every moment of it. That's a piece of you. You are also serious Lydia, who likes to make the world neat and tidy and organized. You like to be in control of your life as much as possible. But you also like stories, magic, and sword fighting beneath the stage. You like to kiss in the moonlight. You are Madame Xyla, as well. You like to read people and understand them. You like to use your skill at cards and observation to dole out advice and give people comfort. At the same time, you like to put on a show and entertain. To shine and dazzle. And I love every one of those things, because each one is a little piece of Lydia. I love all the different pieces, and I love the whole woman they form together."

Lydia gasped. She'd suspected why he was here, and the meaning behind the tulip. Yet somehow the words coming from his lips struck her like a blow to the chest. She could hardly breathe. This was real. He loved her. All of her.

Max hopped up from his seat and began to pace. "That was not how I'd intended this speech to go, but no matter. I know you won't fault me if I get it wrong and have to try again."

Lydia gazed up at him, clutching her tulip over her heart. "It wasn't wrong." Her voice was soft. Vulnerable. So, un-Lydia-like.

Not true. Only a part you keep hidden.

Max's answering smile was lopsided and radiant. "I suppose I should say it again, regardless. I love you, Lydia Weaver. When I'm with you, I feel free. Out in the world I'm never sure of my words. I try to mold myself to be what I'm supposed to be or do what I'm supposed to do, and inevitably I fail and say the wrong thing. But you don't ask me to be anything but what I am. When I'm with you, I can let the words out. I can be odd, silly, joyful, seductive. I can be whatever and whoever I desire."

Tears gathered in the corners of her eyes. Max was saying the words, but they may as well have been written on her heart. Everything he'd said to her, she could say back. How she loved him when he flirted and when he fidgeted. When he laughed and joked. When he strove to help others, even his undeserving father.

"I can always trust you to listen," Max continued.

Lydia's heart jolted.

Oh, God. Oh, God, no. Not that word.

She didn't deserve his trust. Not in any way. He was so honest and open, and she'd deceived him from the start. Deceived herself into believing she could conceal what she was doing without harming him. But it would. She knew it would and she'd hidden it anyway. She'd abused his trust in her and they would both pay for it.

Max didn't notice her sudden agitation, still caught up in what he was saying. "Now I'm trusting you with my heart," he said, sending an unwitting barb straight into her chest. "Will you permit me to court you, Lydia? Not merely for fun, but with the intent to build a future toget—"

"Stop!" she blurted out. She clapped a hand over her mouth. "Oh, Max, please stop. I can't stand it. I can't… I've been so terrible."

He froze for an instant, then rushed to her side, kneeling before her and reaching for her hand.

"Lydia, what's wrong?"

She rose to her feet, brushed past him and strode across the room to her seance table. Blinking back tears, she placed the tulip beside her half-eaten peach. Which flower meant "you are a liar"? That was the only one she deserved.

Calling on the stoic Madame Xyla piece of herself, she slowly turned to face Max.

"I have something I must tell you."

It would be the end of everything. And she had only herself to blame.

22
MAAT
goddess of truth and justice

WHAT HAD HE DONE? What had he said?

Max scrambled to his feet and followed Lydia across the room. His heart raced. He'd known a confession of love came with the risk that she might not return his feelings. But this was something worse. The look on Lydia's face had been one of agony. As if he'd ripped her heart out instead of handing her his.

She turned to face him, now fully composed. Her shoulders had straightened, and her voice rang out calm and clear.

"I have something I must tell you."

Only the trail of a single tear down her cheek revealed the emotions that had been so evident on her face only a moment earlier. Max gaped at her. He'd seen Lydia discipline herself in this manner before, but never so drastically.

"Whatever it is you need to say, you can tell me." He strove to make his voice reassuring, though his body trembled with worry. "Even if you're sad or angry. You don't need to hide your feelings. Not from me. Please don't force yourself to be brave if what you really need is a hand to hold or a shoulder to cry on." He gave her what he hoped was an encouraging smile. "I promise I won't tell anyone."

"No." Lydia gave a quick, sharp shake of the head. "This is the only way." The conviction in her tone couldn't entirely mask the underlying pain. Good Lord, what was wrong?

"Very well." Max took a single step backward and put his hands in his pockets to keep from reaching for her. If she wanted distance between them, she would have it, no matter how he ached to hold her. "Tell me what the trouble is."

"I have a history with your father," Lydia explained, in her placid Madame Xyla voice. "It dates back to when I was a girl. The gambling club my parents owned burned nearly to the ground, leaving Jack and I orphaned. A speculator by the name of Adolphus Millerson swooped in and purchased the remains from under us. We saw no money. As far as I know no one made any attempt to check if the property was held in trust for us. We were nothing to the opportunistic adults."

Max winced. Yes, he could believe that of his father.

"A few years later, we crossed paths with Millerson again. Our skill with cards kept us fed and clothed, but we were not infallible. Jack was caught cheating at one of your father's establishments."

"Damnation," Max muttered. His father irrationally despised card cheats. How many times had he blamed his own mismanagement on people cheating him?

"He could have taken Jack's money and tossed him out. Instead, he accused him of half-a-dozen different crimes. Had him thrown in prison."

"And you were left all alone and afraid," Max whispered. The poor girl. He longed to embrace that younger Lydia. He wanted to reassure her that all wasn't lost. That she and her cousin would both survive and thrive.

"Don't," Lydia snapped, her composure slipping for a moment and a haunted look flashing in her eyes. "Don't pity me. I don't deserve it."

"Because you hate my father? I can't blame you for that. He's selfish and thoughtless. I'd hoped for years he might change if I gave him the right opportunity, but I know now it will never happen."

"You don't understand." Lydia laughed bitterly. "Of course you don't understand. You're too good, and you always seek the good in people. You always write happy endings. But this story doesn't have one."

Max again fought the urge to reach for her. *We can be happy*, he wanted to promise her. *Whatever the hurt in your past, I want to make you happy here in the present and going into the future.*

"I nursed my hatred for years," Lydia continued. "But I was staying alive and trying to build a career, and I had no time for revenge." Her eyes turned away from Max, fixing on a point across the room. "Recently, I learned that the Curiosity Club, built on the remains of my old club, had again come into your father's possession. It was his only remaining investment, people said. If the club failed, he would have nothing. Now I was in a place in my life where I could devote time and resources to avenging my family. All I needed was an opportunity."

Max's stomach dropped. Everything that had happened since the day he'd first walked into this seance room flashed through his mind, the memories realigning one-by-one to form a new and terrible truth.

"Me," he choked out. "I was the opportunity."

He could see it all now, in agonizing clarity. Why she'd turned his pocket change into one thousand pounds in exchange for nothing but entrance to the club. Why she'd accepted a visit to the theater as payment for procuring a mummy. His blood went cold. Christ, but he was a fool.

"You were," she admitted, hitting him with another barb of ice. "I saw a way to learn about the club and took it."

"But why help at all? Why not just let him fail?" Max spoke the words from a distance, barely hearing them over the wailing of his shattered heart.

"I wasn't certain it would be enough. And I wanted to be the one to do it."

"And the mummy's curse?"

"I spread advertisements throughout the club, urging him to hold a spiritualist event. I hadn't considered a mummy unwrapping, but I made use of it. I knew the mummy I brought in would cause a scene, and I paid a man to blame it on a curse if no one else did. I expected smoke or a flash of light, not beetles, but they served their purpose."

"And now you'll be exacting your final revenge." Max couldn't even inflect his words with anger or bitterness. He'd gone numb, unable to feel anything but the endless chasm of his own folly.

"That was the plan," Lydia replied. She touched a pile of papers sitting on the table. "I have it written down right here."

"You do like things organized." Organized. Planned. Plotted. She'd orchestrated an entire scheme around him, and he'd been oblivious. Utterly, ludicrously ignorant. How had he ever thought he'd known her? He couldn't even see what she was doing right in front of his face.

Max pressed a hand to his suddenly throbbing temple.

"I'm so sorry." Lydia's voice wavered almost imperceptibly. "I never wanted to hurt you. I'm so very sorry."

Max tried to form a reply, to make some comment—any comment—on the situation, but nothing would come. No shouting, no crying. Only a gaping maw of nothingness.

"I'm so, so sorry." Tears rolled down Lydia's cheeks, overflowing the dam she'd constructed to hold back her emotions.

A cynical laugh echoed in the back of Max's mind. At least one of them could still feel something.

"I think I ought to go," he said, in the monotone that seemed his only remaining mode of speech.

Lydia dipped her chin. "I'm so sorry," she repeated.

Max believed she was. But no amount of contrition could undo the truth. He'd been a colossal fool and his heart had paid the price. Without another word, he turned and walked away.

23
TEFNET
goddess of moisture

LYDIA TORE OFF A SECTION of her revenge plan and tossed it in the fire. Flames sprouted all across the bit of paper, and it curled in on itself, twisting and writhing as the fire consumed it. She tossed another piece in, watching it burn down to nothing more than a few floating specks of ash. Burning away. Floating away. Like the charred remains of her heart.

You did this to yourself. You betrayed his trust. You broke his heart.

That was the worst part of all. Losing him, she could handle. She'd lost before and survived. But to know that he had lost too, to know *she* had been the cause of his loss, made her physically ill. Somewhere, he was suffering through the same grief she was. And it was all her doing.

If there were some way to undo it, she wouldn't hesitate to take it. She would take all his pain upon herself, where it belonged, and leave him whole and happy.

She tore off another section of notes, part of her diagram marking where all the important players were to have stood.

Lydia paused with her hand outstretched, close enough to the fire that the heat against her skin grew quickly painful. She dropped the paper and withdrew her hand, but the image of her drawing remained in her mind.

Walking away wasn't enough. She needed to undo as much of the damage she'd caused as possible. She could never properly atone for breaking Max's heart, but she could do this.

She could make things the way they should have been, without her interference. Adolphus Millerson would have a chance to reform. A chance he didn't deserve. But Max would have one less worry in his life. That was all that mattered. He might hate her forever, but at least he would know her heart. Even if she never saw him again, he was worth more than her revenge ever could be.

Lydia tossed the rest of the plan into the fire all at once and waited until it had burned away. Time to start anew.

A brisk walk had her arriving at the back entrance to the Enchantment Theatre less than an hour later. She leaned against the wall near the door, prepared to wait as long as necessary for someone to allow her entrance. Or at least tell her where she might find Irving Glastonbury.

The man himself was the first to arrive on the scene, some quarter hour later, sauntering up to her before tipping his top hat in greeting.

"Why, Miss Lydia Weaver! What a pleasure to see you again." He glanced around. "Is Max not here with you?"

For once, Lydia didn't try to conceal her emotions. Better to let Irv see how much she rued her behavior. It would help him understand what needed to be done.

"I don't believe Mr. Millerson is interested in speaking to me any longer."

Irv's eyes grew wide. "What? But he was wild for you."

"I know." Tears gathered in Lydia's eyes again. Someday, when this was over, she would sit down and have a good cry. "I made a terrible mistake and broke his heart. He won't want me back, I'm sure. But there is something I must do for him. When it's done, I promise I'll walk away and never bother him again. But I need assistance, and I was hoping you might be able to help me."

Irv nodded, then slotted a key into the door. "Let's go inside and talk."

～◯

Max clunked his empty glass down on the bar. "'Nother absinthe," he slurred.

The bartender poured some of the green liquid into the glass, dropped in a single sugar cube, and topped it off with a splash of water. Max left a coin on the counter, then staggered back to the couch in the corner where he could sprawl while he cried into his poorly-made drink.

"Disgraceful," he muttered, poking at the sugar cube with a finger. His jabbing did not make the sugar dissolve any faster.

The reason Max liked absinthe was for the ritual around preparing and drinking it. The strange color and the special serving utensils gave the drink a fanciful, almost arcane aura. In a proper absinthe bar, he could let the world slip away. His imagination would wander free as he watched the water dripping from a fountain. *Drip. Drop.* Eating away at the sugar that rested in the slotted spoon above the glass, bit by tiny bit.

Beautiful. Hypnotic. Fitting for a magical drink.

This... Max poked the sugar cube again. This was an abomination. Good for getting soused, though. And appropriate for a world that had had all the magic sucked out of it.

Max lifted the glass. "To the real world," he declared. "Why the bleedin' 'ell anyone would want to live there is beyond me." He brought the drink toward his lips, intending to toss back the offensive concoction in a single gulp.

A large hand clamped down over the glass. Max jerked his head back to avoid getting a mouthful of knuckles. The hand pried the glass from Max's fingers. A second hand appeared, holding a large mug of steaming liquid. The brisk aroma of strong black tea tickled Max's nose.

"Try this instead."

Max looked up from the hands into a familiar face with concerned blue eyes and a wry smile. "Irv?"

"You look more than three sheets to the wind, mate," Irv replied. "Four or five at least. Drink the tea. And move aside so I can sit."

Max blinked up at his friend, then clumsily swung his legs to the floor. Irv shoved the mug of tea into Max's hands, but didn't let go until he had a firm grip on it.

"Drink that. We need to talk."

The mug was warm beneath Max's fingers, the scent of tea enticing. Perhaps it was worth a try. It couldn't be worse than the absinthe.

Irv dropped onto the couch beside Max and took a sip of the green liquid. His mouth twisted.

"Christ, that's revolting! How can you stomach it?" He set the drink aside.

Max lifted one shoulder, then let it drop. He took a sip from the mug. The robust Assam washed away the harsh flavor of the absinthe, leaving behind a soothing heat. Max took another drink. His eyes opened wider.

"I'm exceth—" he slurred. He tried again. "Excessith— Very drunk."

Irv chuckled. "Evidently. But already more alert. Drink your tea. We need to talk."

"Nothing to talk about." Max gulped more tea. Each swallow of the hot liquid cleared a bit of the fog from his mind. He could see better, hear better, think better.

Except he didn't want to think. He'd been drinking to *stop* the thoughts. Which hadn't worked at all. It had only made the thoughts muddled. Maybe tea was better. Tea made his body feel nice, at least.

"Nothing?" Irv echoed, his blond brows arching. "All this brooding is for fun? Have you decided to become a despondent poet? Right. Carry on then." He made as if to rise, then sank back into his seat. "Or does your state of inebriation have something to do with a certain spiritualist?"

"It's everything," Max moaned. "My sister doesn't need

me. My father is a reprobate. I'm unemployed. Lydia doesn't love me. Nothing was real." He glowered at the tea. It was definitely making him more alert. And alert meant facing reality. Everything he'd had with Lydia had been fantasy. Disguises. Fake moonlight. Games and stories. All of it, a trick of his fevered imagination.

"That is extremely melancholy for a man who once told me he wanted to write a version of *Hamlet* where Ophelia's plotline is a carefully constructed ruse and she bursts in at the last minute to save the day."

"Maybe I'll rewrite *The Scribe and the Fortune Teller* to be a tragedy."

Irv shook his head. "Not you. Yes, your life is a bit muddled and you've got the morbs. But you'll recover. Drink more tea. Buck up. You've still got me, haven't you?"

Max gave his friend a half-hearted smile. "I do. Thank you."

"You're welcome." Irv slung an arm around Max's shoulders. "Now, tell me everything."

"Very well."

Max began with the tale of how he'd quit his job, and his subsequent conversation with Lizzie. Once he started, he couldn't seem to stop, though he wasn't sure whether that was because of the alcohol he'd drunk or the sheer relief of unburdening himself. Max didn't bother to try to recall what Irv already knew and what he didn't. Instead, he related the entire sad saga of his relationship with Lydia, from the moment he'd first laid eyes on her. He did, however, omit a few of the more intimate details.

Partway through the recounting, his tea ran out and Irv fetched him a second mug. By the time Max reached the part of the tale where he made his ill-advised confession of love, this second helping of tea was also gone, and he was feeling vastly more sober. He summarized Lydia's plan of revenge, then slumped against the back of the couch and closed his eyes.

Even the comfort of having a confidant couldn't ease the pain of that memory.

"I was such a fool," he lamented.

"Rubbish," Irv sniffed. "I heard nothing foolish in your entire story. You left a job you hated, you told off your father the way you've wanted to do for years, you cleared up a misunderstanding with your sister, and you fell in love with an interesting, intelligent woman. It's only natural to be emotional after some serious, honest conversation. Not foolish in the least. Now it's time to clean yourself up and go win the lady."

Max opened his eyes and sat up straight. "Did you hear nothing I said? None of it was real. She doesn't love me. I was only an opportunity for revenge."

"Are you certain about that? Let's apply a bit of logic to the situation, shall we? Did she say, 'Max, I don't love you'?"

"No, of course not. She's not cruel. She was very apologetic."

"Ah. So she must like you."

Max stared at his friend for a moment. The last thing he wanted to do was continue to dwell on a hopeless situation, but he couldn't deny that Irv made an excellent point. Max had been too busy being consumed by heartbreak to stop and reflect on what had transpired. Maybe this was what he needed. Maybe calmly analyzing the situation would give him enough perspective to move on.

"Yes, I'm sure she did like me, but not in the way I had imagined," he replied.

Irv rubbed his chin. "Perhaps. She didn't know you at all when she began her revenge, of course."

"No, of course not." How could she have? And she couldn't have known from that first meeting that such a strong spark of attraction would grow between them. She hadn't set out to make him fall in love. Lydia would never do such a thing. That had all been Max's fault.

"Right. And now that she *does* know you?"

Max rubbed his temple where a headache was beginning to form. "What of it?"

"Did she simply forge ahead with her original plan, entirely ignoring you?" Irv prompted.

"Well… no. She confessed everything." Why *had* she done that? She must have decided Max deserved to know the truth. She'd been sincere when she'd apologized for hurting him. But he couldn't decipher what she might have been thinking. His heart ached too much, and he still wasn't entirely sober.

"I ought to tell you that I had a most interesting conversation with her a short time ago," Irv admitted.

Max jerked. "You did what?"

"She came by the theater. She's planning some sort of spiritual cleansing of a gaming club. Removing a curse. Making the place lucky again, or what-have-you. She wanted an assistant to help. Would you know anything about that?"

"She… But…" Max shook his head. "She wants to ruin the club. You must have misunderstood."

Irv's grin was almost wicked. "Really? Because she gave me a script for a ghostly voice." He produced a paper and waved it about. "Does 'may luck shine upon you' sound like ruin?"

Max had a sudden sense that he must have hallucinated this entire conversation. He ought never to have drunk the questionable absinthe. Lydia wouldn't uncurse the club. She wouldn't help his father. It made no sense.

"You ought to go after your girl, mate," Irv said, softly, but earnestly. "I know you love her, and I'd wager good money she loves you too."

Max shook his head, still unable to process this new information. He was dreaming. He'd passed out from drink. That had to be it.

"You're not going to let a silly thing like revenge stand in the way of true love, are you?" Irv asked. "You? Master of the Feisty Fairy Tale?"

"No," Max replied, without hesitation. This dream was

better than reality. He could be the hero and trample all that stood between himself and his happy ending.

"Brilliant. I have to get back to the theater now." Irv took hold of Max's arm and helped him up from the couch. The room swayed. "Let's get you home to sleep this off. Tomorrow when you're clear-headed, I'll tell you everything I know and you'll make a plan for how to capture your lady's heart."

"I will?" Max let Irv steer him toward the exit. His unsteady gait and spinning head felt too substantial to be a hallucination. Could real-world Max face Lydia again? Could he dare to risk himself after pain and heartbreak, in the slim hope she would have more than mild affection for him? It didn't seem likely.

The memory of Irv's confident voice echoed in his head. *Rubbish!*

He was right. Real world Max had told his father to stuff it. He'd quit his job in a fit of pique. Maybe real world Max was braver than he seemed.

"Yes," he declaimed, in a too-loud, still-a-bit-drunk voice. "I will."

24
PETBE
goddess of revenge

Lydia surveyed the small crowd assembled in the main card room of the Curiosity Club. The men were gathered in a tight semicircle around her, leaving perhaps three-quarters of the room empty. A tiny event, compared to the mummy unwrapping. Fortunately, several reporters lurked among the attendees today, sitting with pen and paper poised.

Julian Carter was also in attendance, here at Lydia's invitation. He'd been looking to buy the club for a song. She might have some apologizing to do and an extra favor owed, if things went the way she planned. So be it.

A single overhead light illuminated the small table where Lydia sat, as well as the sphinx fountain behind her. A young man walked a circle around the room, turning off all the other lamps.

Across the table, Adolphus Millerson fidgeted, shifting his weight in a way so familiar that a new pang of loss struck Lydia's heart. If only Max were here. She longed to apologize again, and more profusely. She wanted him to see what she was doing here today, rather than hear about it later. But this was the way it had to be. It would be easier to walk away if she didn't have to see him.

The last of the lights went out, and Millerson leaned forward, bringing himself within Lydia's sphere of light. He wore a pinched expression, and dark circles beneath both eyes suggested restless nights. Good. Lydia might have abandoned her quest for vengeance, but this man deserved to feel the weight of his folly. She wouldn't destroy him, but neither would she forgive him for what he'd done to her family or for the way he'd taken advantage of his son's generosity.

Lydia closed her eyes and let her body relax. When she spoke, her voice was clear and loud, but with the soothing undertones she'd perfected from years at her profession.

"The air is troubled," she declared. "I feel the vibrations, the currents of uneasy spirits." An imperceptible movement of her hand made the table rock. When setting up, she'd checked over every chair in the room and employed all the wobbly ones as audience seating. Anyone susceptible would feel their own vibrations.

"If those gathered here are believers, then we may call the spirits forth and learn what troubles them. Any who do not believe must depart now."

No one left, of course. They never did.

Lydia began a modified version of her standard seance ritual, asking the audience to close their eyes and relax.

"Open your minds and your hearts," she told the crowd. "For it is only when we welcome the spirits with pure intent that they will speak."

She was such a liar. A swindler. As bad as the shell game man on the street. She spoke of purity and honesty while she deceived everyone. Her heartache was well-earned indeed.

Despite her self-recrimination, she proceeded with the seance in her usual professional manner. She spoke on behalf of the spirits, reiterating their unease and speaking of troubling changes and unsettling events.

Across the table, Millerson rocked in his seat and clenched his jaw, his agitation growing. Thus far, Lydia had yet to deviate from her original plan. Millerson, like everyone in the audience, would understand the implication that his ridiculous renovations and the chaos of the mummy unwrapping were to blame.

"The fountain!" someone cried.

Ah. Right on time.

"The fountain!" the man shouted again. "It's spouting blood!"

It wasn't blood. It was a simple dye. Her lamplighter boy had done his job admirably. Lydia kept her expression impassive, but inside she was smiling.

Maybe she was more Fun and Playful Lydia than she'd acknowledged, because this was her favorite part of the event. Perhaps it would have made sense to eliminate it when she'd adapted to uncurse the club, but she'd liked it too much. And all the best spiritual events contained a healthy amount of spectacle.

"Spirits!" she called out. "Reveal yourselves to us. Speak, that we may learn how to bring you peace."

"There can be no peace." The voice rumbled across the ceiling, deep and furious.

Lydia flinched. This was not in the script. Irv was supposed to play a spirit, calling out for her assistance. She would coax the audience to think freeing thoughts, and when the fountain ran clear again, she would declare the spirits released from their burden.

"A curse is upon this house," the voice upstairs continued. The sound trembled throughout the room, more spectral than Lydia could have imagined. "A curse born of folly and immoderation."

Murmurs rose from the audience. Across the table, Adolphus Millerson had gone pale. Lydia's fingers clenched. What was happening?

"A curse *you* have brought upon us."

Max? Hell and damnation, was that Max's voice? Elation coursed through her, quickly followed by a burst of anger. What did he think he was doing?

"You," the voice declared again. "You with your arrogance

and misplaced pride, have made a mockery of what was once our safe haven."

Lydia's whole face tightened as she fought a scowl. That was definitely Max, and he was turning everything upside down. She'd come here to put things right, but instead she was getting her revenge, carefully targeted and executed. And, of course, his words were better than those she might have used.

"Heed our words, foolish one," Max continued, "for your path is a path to ruin. Heed us as you have failed to heed the words of those close to you."

This script was perfect. Everyone in the room would be staring at the man across the table from her, who was trembling now. His cheeks had gone from ashen to scarlet. He recognized that the words were directed at him, and anyone watching would see it.

Goddammit, Maxwell Millerson.

Lydia wanted to scream at him for so entirely destroying any hope of restoring things to the way they'd once been. At the same time, she wanted to fling her arms around him and kiss him for his brilliance and daring.

Max's father leapt to his feet, knocking his chair to the ground. "You ungrateful brat!" he shouted at the ceiling. "How dare you do this to me?"

"Heed this warning," Max commanded, "for it will be your last."

Adolphus Millerson shook his fist in the air. "I am your father! Do you hear me!"

The buzzing of the crowd had grown to a full-on clamor.

"It's all a hoax!" a voice shouted from the darkness.

"But the fountain!" another man insisted. "There's blood in the fountain!"

More voices jumped in to argue with them. Half-a-dozen at least began yelling at Adolphus, either demanding answers or telling him to sit down and shut up.

Lydia's teeth clenched. She had lost control. The deed was done and she could only sit and watch the aftermath.

Upstairs, Max continued to talk, ordering his father to leave town and never return. He didn't do things by half-measures, her Max. Her grand atonement was well and truly ruined, damn him. Lovely, exasperating man.

Max's father stomped his foot in absolute rage. "How could you be so unfeeling? I am your family! Your own flesh and blood!"

Lydia sprang from her seat. She stomped around the table, seized Adolphus by his coat and snarled, "You don't deserve him. You *never* deserved him." She shoved her enemy away, directly into the arms of a man with a notebook.

"Mr. Millerson," the reporter said cheerily. "What have you to say about this incident?"

"How long has your son's ghost been haunting you?" asked another.

Newspapermen swarmed around him, and Lydia stormed off through the sea of confused and excited spectators. She didn't deserve Max either, but she had to see him. He'd come for her. Despite her lies and manipulations, he'd come for her.

Lydia's heart beat erratically and her hands shook. Dread and hope tangled inside her, twisting her stomach into knots. She had her revenge, but the victory was hollow. Worthless. He'd ruined everything. How could she show him now that she was sorry? How could she ever prove that he meant more to her than any vengeance could? That he meant everything to her.

Lifting her skirts, Lydia scurried up the stairs to the secret passage. The door was well-concealed, and she had to run her hands up and down the paneling to find the latch.

As the door swung open, she steeled herself with a calming breath. Max lay on the floor of the narrow passage, his ear pressed to a large cone, listening to the commotion below. Her breath stuttered at the sight of him.

The door swung closed, plunging them into darkness.

25
MIN

god of love and sexual pleasure

MAX SCRAMBLED TO HIS FEET. He could see enough from the light seeping through the spy slits in the passage walls to make out the shape of a woman. And only one woman would have come looking for him in this hidden corridor.

"Lydia?" he whispered, stepping cautiously forward, trying not to make a sound. Given the commotion downstairs, no one was likely to hear, but Max preferred to take care, regardless. If Lydia was here to talk, he didn't want to be interrupted.

"What are you *doing*?" she hissed.

"What am *I* doing?" Max pressed forward until Lydia's skirts brushed his legs. He flattened his hands against the door to either side of her, leaning in to keep his voice as low as possible. "I am attempting to set everything right."

"Right?" Her voice rose in pitch, a barely audible squeak of outrage. "You've ruined my plan!"

"I've fixed it," Max insisted.

Lydia's hot, angry breath scorched his skin. He couldn't see her eyes, even at this distance, but he knew they would be sharp as blue ice.

"No. *I* was fixing it," she snarled. "I was restoring everything to the way it should have been. I was undoing all my meddling. And now… Now…"

Her voice broke, the quivering words heavy with pain and uncertainty. Max almost embraced her, his heart pounding with the need to soothe and reassure. She didn't show Vulnerable

Lydia to anyone—not even herself, he suspected. This was twice, now, that he'd glimpsed that facet of her, and this time he wasn't going to run away because of his own worries.

"Why do it?" he whispered gently. "Why give up something you'd worked so hard for?"

Max knew the answer. He studied people as part of his writing. Once he'd stepped out of his grief and assessed her actions, her motive had become abundantly clear. But he needed to hear it from her. They couldn't move forward with things unspoken.

"Because I hurt you!" Her fist thumped against his shoulder, hard enough to convey her frustration without doing damage. "I hurt you and I couldn't undo that. But I needed to atone. I needed to make things better."

"Why?" he murmured.

Lydia grabbed hold of his coat and dragged him closer. "Because I love you, you mush-head!"

Max cupped her face in his hands and bent to press his forehead to hers. Warm, wet tears trickled down her cheeks to where his fingers rested against her skin. For a long moment he stayed frozen in place, letting himself simply feel her, breathe her, hold her.

"Say that again," he sighed.

Her fingers unclenched, flattening against his chest. "Mush-head," she repeated.

Max tipped her chin up and brushed his lips over hers. "You love me."

"Yes." More tears dripped down her cheeks. "I do. I wanted to show you revenge no longer mattered. I only wanted you."

"Next time you can tell me. I like words."

Lydia let out a soft laugh. "Mine aren't as polished as yours. Your pretty speeches make me all mawkish. Me! And now you've eviscerated your father."

"It had to be done. And I had to be the one to do it." The truth of the words settled in his chest. He'd needed this. A clear, unequivocal, public break. Whatever his father did from this point on, Max's part in it was over. "I didn't need you to turn the clock back. I needed to move forward. Thank you for the opportunity."

A choked sound escaped Lydia's throat. She felt the weight of that word.

Max wrapped his arms tightly around her. "Maybe our first meeting was a different opportunity than you realized. For something bigger than each of us alone. Do you remember what you said about The Lovers card? 'To find the peace you seek, you must be open to cooperation. Look for the one who will join you.' Will you join me, love?"

Her kiss was so swift and so intense Max almost staggered. She buried her fingers in his hair, pulling him tight to her, claiming him with bold, ravenous strokes.

Max melted into the unfettered passion that was Lydia. This was who she was. Expressing her deepest, truest feelings was no easy task for her. And when they did rise to the surface, she preferred actions to words.

He could work with that.

He returned her kiss with all the vigor and yearning she had begun it with. Their mouths crashed and their tongues twisted, stroke-for-stroke, taste-for-taste. Max crushed her against the door, melding their bodies together, writhing against her in sudden, desperate need.

Lydia's lips caressed his jaw, then pressed a scorching kiss to his neck. "Lord, Max," she groaned. "I'd thought I'd never see you again." She yanked at his collar to expose more of his throat. "I'd thought I'd never taste you again."

His hands began to move, up and down her body, remembering her curves, etching them on his heart. "I drunk myself silly," he answered. "When we could have been doing this."

Lydia's hands dropped from his shirt to his trousers. "I need you," she panted. "I need you now."

This was madness. Up against the door, in a cramped secret passage, where anyone downstairs or outside might hear. Utter madness.

So why was Max yanking up her skirts? Why was he smothering her moans with more merciless kisses? God, he hoped the door was sturdy enough.

He lifted her up, and she wrapped her legs around him, clinging to him as he braced them both against the door. When he sank into her glorious wet heat, he groaned audibly.

"Shh." Lydia rocked her hips. "Shh."

Max didn't know whether she was talking to herself or to him. It was hard to think of anything, honestly, except how damn good she felt around him.

Here, in the darkness and the silence, it was impossible to tell her everything that was in his heart. He could only follow her lead, and let his body do the talking.

You are mine, he told her with every powerful thrust, every muffled sound. *My love. My only.*

And you are mine, her body responded. Strong hands held him in an unwavering grip. Eager lips branded his skin. His name escaped her throat, a plea for release.

When she found it, her whole body convulsed in ecstasy, and she groaned her pleasure into his kiss. His goddess of the moon. Brilliant even in pure darkness. Max thrust deep one final time and let himself join her in sublime release.

Panting, he set her back on her feet and sagged against the door, cradling her in his arms. Her fingers slid soft strokes up and down his back.

"I love you," she whispered.

Max's heart swelled near to bursting. "I love you too."

He wanted to stay where he was, holding her and kissing her, but they had already taken an enormous risk. It was time to leave this gaming house before their luck turned.

"What say we go somewhere I can hold you all night and

we can make as much noise as we like? Your house, perhaps, where my father won't know to look."

Lydia answered with a rustling of fabric, presumably setting herself to rights as best she could. Max fastened his trousers and smoothed down his hair with his hands. It would do.

Hand-in-hand, they slipped from the passage, blinking in the bright light of the gas lamps. Footsteps pounded up the stairs toward them.

"I know you're up there, boy!" Max's father shouted.

Max tugged Lydia in the opposite direction. "We'll slip out the servant's entrance."

They raced to the back stairs, half-running, half-jumping down, before stumbling out the rear door into the alley behind the club.

"You two had a jolly time up there, aye?" a smooth tenor voice commented.

Max spun to discover a slight, redheaded man leaning against the wall, smoking a cigar. He tipped his hat to them.

"Thank you for the spectacle, Madame Xyla," he continued. "I think I'll buy this club. Consider my favor returned in full."

Lydia gave him a curt nod. "Please excuse us, Mr. Carter. We have a prior engagement." She squeezed Max's hand and led him away at a brisk walk.

"Or perhaps a future engagement?" Max suggested, as they turned out of the alley.

The only indication he'd startled her was a tiny twitch. "That depends. Are you planning to propose?"

"Yes, if you're amenable. I already gave you a grand confession of love. It ought to be easier the second time around."

"I haven't any more revenge plots to confess, so you're safe." She pursed her lips in thought. "Although there is the problem of your name. I don't want to be a Millerson."

Max waved his free hand nonchalantly. "I certainly won't insist upon it. I can call you Mrs. Weaver and everyone can assume you're my scandalous mistress." He started around a corner.

Lydia resisted. "That's not the way to my house."

"No. But it *is* the way to Covent Garden. We might find a flower seller still working this time of night."

The streetlamp was just bright enough to show the flush of pleasure that rose to her cheeks.

"Very well. Proceed."

A short walk later, a grubby girl with a basket of bedraggled blooms provided Max with the necessary foliage. He picked out all the best violets and presented them to his lady love.

"Violets. A symbol of enduring faithfulness. A good way to begin a marriage, I'd say."

Lydia tucked one flower behind each ear, then arranged the rest in her décolletage. "What do you think?"

"Perfect. Now come this way." He drew her down a street where the gas lamps had either gone out or never been lit to begin with.

"You intend to get us attacked by footpads?" she teased.

Max scowled. "If anyone interrupts this, I will pound him into the pavement."

"Not if I do it first."

He laughed and pulled her into his arms. "This is dark enough." He pointed upward, to the silvery moon that hung in the night sky. "My moonlight nymph," he began. "My dazzling seeress. My practical planner and my flirtatious friend. I adore you with every beat of my heart, every breath I take. Would you accept my hand in marriage, that I might also call you my wife?"

Lydia kissed him.

Quite a bit later, she added, "Yes. I love you, too."

26
ISIS

goddess of marriage, magic, and wisdom

LYDIA WOKE AT HER USUAL TIME to the smell of cooking breakfast. As far as her cook knew, she would be down to eat according to her usual schedule.

She wasn't.

Rising from bed was much more difficult with a handsome man beside you, looking adorably disheveled and smiling in a way that made your insides turn to jelly. Lydia couldn't help but linger. She needed to see him, needed to touch him. This was real. He'd forgiven her misdeeds, professed to still love her, and offered his hand in marriage. He was hers.

When she finally did force herself from the bed, she dressed simply, in a blue that matched her eyes. No jewelry. Nothing in her hair. Last night had been wild, and today she was in the mood for peace. Max called her lovely, as he always did.

Downstairs, Jack and Tess sat at the table, finishing their own breakfast. Phantom sat beside baby Alex, gobbling up the scraps she'd scattered all over. Lydia had intended to spend the entire day with them, since they were scheduled to leave tomorrow. She would need to inform them that their family had added a member.

Jack looked up from the newspaper when Lydia and Max entered.

"Morning, Lydia," he said brightly. He nodded at Max. "Millerson. You're alive after all."

"I, um… yes," Max replied.

Jack laid the paper on the table and tapped his finger to an article. "According to this, I ought to be photographing you for my spirit images." He cleared his throat and read. "'Club Owner Haunted by Son's Ghost: Mummified Remains Responsible for Run of Bad Luck?' Care to explain what happened last night?"

Lydia took a seat. "May I see the paper, please?"

Jack pushed it toward her. "Enjoy. A lot of sensationalist rubbish, if you ask me."

Tess poked her husband. "I used to write for that newspaper, if you recall."

"Yes, well, they appear to be suffering without you." Jack rested both elbows on the table in a deliberate display of poor manners. "But what I really want to hear about is how did you two come to be here together this morning, looking all happy and smitten with one another?"

Lydia folded the newspaper neatly in front of her. "Max ruined my attempt to give up my revenge out of love for him. I have determined that the only suitable retaliation is to wed him."

Jack's radiant smile made Lydia's heart sing. "Brilliant! I'm sorry we won't be able to stay long enough to be part of your wedding. But I will give you the name of a capable photographer."

Lydia's shoulders sagged. She wanted her family here when she married. But she couldn't ask Jack to stay any longer, and she didn't want to wait until he was able to visit again.

"We could marry today, if time is a consideration," Max suggested. Everyone at the table turned to stare at him. "It wouldn't be legally binding, of course, but I'm sure I could talk someone at the theater into setting up the stage for us, and we could conduct a small ceremony."

Lydia leapt from her seat, flung her arms around Max, and kissed him. "Yes, oh, yes!" she cried. "Oh, Max, that would be perfect!"

"Damn," Jack breathed. "I haven't seen that level of

excitement from Lydia in ages. Well done, Millerson. You absolutely have my blessing. Welcome to the family."

Max beamed and kissed Lydia again.

Later that day, Lydia and Max exchanged vows on the stage of the Enchantment Theatre. Surrounding them were Lydia's family, a curious black cat, the ladies of ILSA, Max's sister Lizzie, and an assortment of actors and stagehands. Irving Glastonbury, dressed in a ridiculous brown monk's robe, presided over the festivities. Jack documented it all with his camera. The wedding was whimsical, raucous, entirely unofficial, and perfect.

Beneath the artificial moonlight, the nymph kissed her poet husband. This would forever be her real wedding day.

Epilogue
Thoth
god of the moon, writing, and scribes

7 months later

Max wiped away a stray tear. All around him, the audience was rising to its feet, whistling and clapping their approval. Down on the stage, Irv took his final bows, the radiant smile on his face entirely unrehearsed. Max would be sending him a large bottle of brandy as a thank you. *The Scribe and the Fortune Teller* was an opening night sensation.

Lydia flung her arms around him in a fierce hug. For propriety's sake, she lingered only a moment, but even so brief a public display was a bold statement of her pleasure.

"It was wonderful!" She applauded and waved to the actors down on the stage. "I'm so proud of you and so proud of everyone involved."

"Great fun," agreed Lizzie, who stood at Max's other side. "Thank you for bringing me to see it before I left town."

"You're most welcome," Max replied. "Any time you'd like to see a show, you need only send word. You're always welcome to stay with me and Lydia if you'd like to visit town."

"Of course I'll come to visit!" Lizzie exclaimed. "London will always be only a train ride away. And I will need to visit Papa as well," she added, with less enthusiasm.

Max harrumphed. He wasn't yet ready to speak to his father again. Someday he would, but today was not that day.

"They're happily settled into the new house," Lizzie informed him.

"Or perhaps, 'conveniently settled'?" Max suggested. After selling the club to pay off his debts, Adolphus Millerson had chosen the classic escape for a penniless man: marry a wealthy widow.

"Our new stepmother delights in ordering him about. Papa seems resigned to his fate. I think they are strangely well-matched."

Max reached for Lydia's hand. He knew what it was to be truly well-matched. To love and respect one's spouse. She twined her fingers with his. Partners.

"I ought to be going," Lizzie declared. "I can't be out too late, with all the packing that needs to be completed for my move. But have fun chatting with the actors, or whatever it is you do now." She gave Max a kiss on the cheek. "Goodnight, brother dear."

Max resisted the urge to insist she stay rather than taking a cab all on her own. Not being the family protector was a continuous adjustment. "Goodnight, Lizzie."

After her departure, Max and Lydia sauntered out into the hall, where the happy crowd chatted and mingled. Max couldn't help listening in on conversations, both eager and terrified to know what people had to say about his latest creation.

"Utterly unrealistic, in my opinion," one man griped. "Why not marry the prince? That scribe was nobody."

"It was so romantic," another enthused. "I was absolutely swept away!"

"I would swear I've seen a fortune-telling act exactly like the one in the play," a third person remarked.

Lydia chuckled at that last. "They did do an excellent job with the seance scene, didn't they?"

"Absolutely," Max agreed. "Thank you for leading the cast through those demonstrations."

"My pleasure, love."

"Irgrimm!" a booming voice called out. "Fabulous play! Well done!"

Max flushed as faces all through the room turned to look at him. He'd been much more public with his nom de plume of late, but notoriety remained unexpected and awkward.

"Name's Pilson," the man who'd called Max's name said. "You may have seen my theater column in the papers. Doing a write up on this one tonight. Do you have anything you'd like to say, as the author of this particular play?"

"Only that I am thrilled with the work of the entire cast and crew, and I thank them for a stellar performance."

"Of course, of course." The reporter looked at Lydia. "And you must be the mysterious Mrs. Weaver. Is it true you and Mr. Irgrimm are secretly married?"

Lydia gave him her aloof spiritualist smile. "One cannot reveal secrets and remain mysterious, sir. Therefore, I must decline to comment on any connection between myself and my friend."

"And what have you to say?" the man asked Max.

Max shook his head. "I would never contradict a lady." He gave the reporter a nod. "I'm afraid I must return to work. Please excuse us."

It wasn't entirely a pretext. Max wanted to check in with the cast and crew, in case there were any logistical changes that needed to be made before the next performance. The Enchantment Theatre, it had turned out, had been in dire need of organizational assistance. Max had stepped easily into the role, handling the mail, keeping track of accounts, managing deliveries, and many other things he'd done at his previous position. The pay was less, but the hours were shorter, he liked the people, and he wasn't bored. No one berated him if he paused for an hour here and there to write. And since the theater didn't operate on typical business hours, Max could match his schedule to Lydia's.

They slipped backstage to talk and celebrate with the actors and stage crew. The mood was universally light. The show had gone off with only minor missteps, the audience was pleased, the owner was pleased, and Max was incandescent with happiness. A successful show and his lady by his side. What could be better?

Eventually, the excitement began to wind down. Irv was gathering a group to go for drinks at the pub, but Lydia waved him off, yawning.

"Could we head for home?" she asked, resting her head on Max's shoulder.

It wasn't terribly late, but it had been a busy day. Quiet time at home with his wife sounded exactly right.

"I think that's a fine idea," he replied.

Through some miracle of fate, they managed to hail a cab within a matter of minutes, and were soon bouncing down the streets, snuggled together, away from prying eyes.

Lydia lifted a hand to Max's cheek, turning his head so she could press a long, tender kiss to his lips. "Now I can properly congratulate you on a job well done."

Max slid an arm around her shoulders. "Thank you, love. You know you were my muse."

Her eyes gleamed with pleasure. "And you know I'd choose you over any prince. As far as I'm concerned, our fairy tale is the best."

"Oh, absolutely. After all, we've had curses, ghosts, revenge, heartache, sacrifice, true love. I can only imagine what else lies in store."

Lydia placed a hand to her belly, rubbing in a slow circle. Max's heart skipped a beat.

"Soon I'll have your first-born child, like you promised me," she murmured. "Then, who can say? What happens after 'happily ever after'?"

Max pressed a soft kiss into her hair. "The show goes on. I write more plays, Madame Xyla sees more clients, our babies grow up." He lifted his wife into his lap, holding her close. Cheek-to-cheek. Heart-to heart. "And there live we, as merry as the day is long."

THE END

ABOUT THE AUTHOR

Award-winning author Catherine Stein believes that everyone deserves love and that Happily Ever After has the power to help, to heal, and to comfort. She writes sassy, sexy romance set during the Victorian and Edwardian eras. Her stories are full of action, adventure, magic, and fantastic technologies.

Catherine lives in Michigan with her husband and three rambunctious kids. She loves steampunk and Oxford commas, and can often be found dressed in Renaissance festival clothing, drinking copious amounts of tea.

Visit Catherine online at

www.catsteinbooks.com

and join her VIP mailing list for a free short story.

Follow her on Twitter @catsteinbooks,
or like her page on Facebook @catsteinbooks.

ALSO BY CATHERINE STEIN

Potions and Passions

The Earl on the Train - Book 0.5

How to Seduce a Spy - Book 1

Mishaps & Mistletoe -
A Holiday Novella -Book 1.5

Not a Mourning Person - Book 2

Once a Rake, Always a Rogue - Book 3

Love at Second Sight - Book 4

Sass and Steam

Love is in the Airship - Book 0.5

A Shot to the Heart - Book 0.75

Eden's Voice - Book 1

What Are You Doing New Year's Eve? –
A Holiday Novella - Book 1.5

Priceless - Book 2

Dead Dukes Tell No Tales - Book 3

Arcane Tales

The Scoundrel's New Con - Book 1

Other Books

Mating Habits - Book 1

Idle Nature - Book 2

Available at your favorite online retailer.
www.catsteinbooks.com

~⌒

Thank you so much for reading.
If you enjoyed the book and are so inclined, I would love for you to leave a review. Happy readers make an author's day!

I love hearing from readers,
so feel free to contact me on social media, or email:

catherine@catsteinbooks.com

~⌒